bushfire

bushfire
stories of lesbian desire

edited by karen barber

ALYSON PUBLICATIONS
LOS ANGELES

Cover photo by Sharon Speller.

Manufactured in the United States of America.
Printed on acid-free paper.

This trade paperback original is published by Alyson Publications Inc.,
P.O. Box 4371, Los Angeles, California 90078-4371.
Distributed in the United Kingdom by Turnaround Publisher Services Ltd.,
Unit 3 Olympia Trading Estate, Coburg Road, Wood Green,
London N22 6TZ, England.

First edition: December 1991

10 9 8 7 6 5

ISBN 1-55583-312-8
(Previously published with the same ISBN by Lace Publications, an imprint of
Alyson Publications Inc.)

Credits
"A True Story (Whether You Believe It or Not)" appeared in slightly different form
in *Secrets,* short stories by Lesléa Newman. Copyright © 1990 by New Victoria
Publishers. Reprinted with permission of the author and publisher.

"A Letter of Apology to Ms. Alice" appeared in slightly different form in *Sinister
Wisdom* 25, Winter 1984.

"Long Distance" appeared in slightly different form in *Field Guide to Outdoor
Erotica.* Copyright © 1988 by Solstice Press.

For Susan,
my HBSP,
always

Contents

✦✦✦✦

Introduction

✦✦✦✦

It is my hope that by naming this collection *Bushfire* I've successfully captured how I feel about lesbian sex: it's hip, it's hot, and, not unimportantly, it's fun.

I was pleasantly amused by the wide range of reactions I received when I told various women this book's name. Some women were shocked, some laughed, and some thought it was just plain rude. I now realize just how different lesbians are from each other and how many of those differences revolve around sex. We come into our sexuality from different places, and we certainly express it in different ways. But *Bushfire*, as a collection of lesbian fiction, is not about analyzing what makes us hot and why. Instead, the stories are about women seeking pleasure, whether from a specific woman, a particular type of woman, or, in some tales, *any* woman. Having sex, or wanting sex, with women is what makes us lesbians. *This* is what *Bushfire* is about: lesbian desire.

Several motifs will become apparent as you begin reading through this anthology. In the lyrical "Turtlehawk Dreams an Ocean Breathing," Lynne Yamaguchi Fletcher uses the hot Arizona sun to set up the rising heat between two new friends, heat that ignites a fire only the ocean can extinguish. Catherine Houser's "Sweat" offers us steamy sex in a sauna with an orange as a sex toy. If Anita Bryant only knew — they're not just for breakfast anymore!

Add an ocean to the sun's oppressive heat and you have Rita Speicher's "Long Distance," a story that exudes desire to the very end. In "Sea Witch," by Patricia Roth Schwartz, an overworked woman finds comfort in an oceanfront women's inn, only to have her serenity interrupted by an unexpected visitor. Keeping with the water imagery, we move from oceans to canals with Alana Corsini's "Also an Island," where passion flows and ebbs with the Venetian rains.

"The Helper" and "Window-Shopping" are sex stories, pure and simple. Molly Martin illustrates that we don't need spoken words to express our desires and Michele LaMarca offers hope to all the closeted secretaries in corporate America who fantasize about their co-workers.

It's happy trails to you in Pam McArthur's "Me and Charlie and Her," a playful romp through the stables with an equestrian triangle. "Habits," by Willyce Kim, is a slick piece about a birthday girl with an obsession for nuns and the call girl who is willing to answer her prayers. And a self-described "proper old-fashioned stone-bulldyke" is in for the surprise of her life when a mysterious, high-heeled femme breezes into town in Lesléa Newman's "A True Story (Whether You Believe It or Not)."

The butch-femme motif is explored again in Dorothy Love's "A Letter of Apology to Ms. Alice," as one woman naively describes to another the only exposure she's had to "womens loving on womens" — in graphic sexual detail. SDiane Bogus gives us "Down-Home Blues," a captivating look at an older African-American woman's second sexual awakening, set against the background of old-time blues and the old-time butch-femme culture of the Deep South.

I included Donna Marie Nowak's "Underground Fame" because I became entranced by the characters she crafted in this dark tale of life in the underbelly of New Orleans. She reminds us that hot sex isn't always salvation; some people just don't want to be saved. Conversely, Jane Futcher's "Past Lives" powerfully illustrates how a loving relationship can enable a woman to confront the past and heal. And Diane Ferry's "The Merry Widow," a bittersweet remembrance of a lover — and a moment — now gone, makes a good case along the way for black lace and for making hets sweat. You'll see what I mean.

Bushfire ends with Wendy Caster's "Spelunking," a hilarious look at the politics of penetration. Remember, lesbian sex is supposed to be fun.

Finally, I'd like to thank a few people who made this book possible. Of course, I need to thank Sasha Alyson for trusting me with the project. I also thank my lover, Susan, for everything; Tina Portillo for offering advice, giving me a fresh perspective on things, and reading manuscripts; everyone at Alyson Publications who listened to me whine; Cathy Houser, for many, many things, including encouragement and criticism; and Lynne Y. Fletcher, whose knowledge, insights, and expertise truly made this book happen. I cannot thank you all enough.

Karen Barber
July 1991

Turtlehawk dreams an ocean breathing

✦✦✦✦ *Lynne Yamaguchi Fletcher*

When did wanting to kiss her turn to certainty that I would? When I turned from an eight-foot-tall painting of purple coyotes dancing in a red-and-orange night to find her watching me, the flecks in her eyes flashing green across the gallery, the tip of her tongue seeking the corner of her half-smile like a shadow nudging light.

We had spent the day together, meeting at eight in the parking lot at the base of Squaw Peak to make the climb before the heat became too intense. In another few weeks, eight would be a late start, but this early in May, the daily high hadn't yet broken a hundred, and we could count on getting up and back at a leisurely pace without frying.

We took our time hiking up, stepping aside to let by the backpackers-in-training and the runners, some on their second or third trip up or down. We talked as we walked, about, literally, everything under the sun — the chollas haloed in the morning light, the hummingbirds sipping the first waxy blooms of the saguaros, the city spreading its turquoise finery — backyard pools — below us as we climbed higher and higher, her growing up in the desert, my hopscotch

journey here, her pending divorce, my editing, her teaching —
one subject segueing into the next like morning into day.

She fascinated me. It wasn't her looks, though she was
pretty enough, with a lively face under a cap of hair four
shades lighter than my near-black, lit with random strands that
shone golden in the sun. Rather, it was the conviction of her
charm that drew me, the aura she projected, at once naive and
seductive, of a child-woman certain of her allure. She didn't
need a model's physique to claim womanhood; her being —
pale, petite, and succulent — proclaimed it. Sex was an
attitude with her, an angle of eye, a line of throat, a language
she spoke with assurance and, one was sure, fluently, though
she dropped only a word or two, perfectly pronounced, here
and there into conversation.

Winded and exhilarated from the final, vertical climb, we
lingered an hour at the top of Squaw Peak, longer than we'd
planned, sprawled on a rock face, basking in our bodies,
taking in the Sunday-blue sky with what we'd learned about
each other. We'd spanned a range of feeling in our conversation, shifting fluidly from solemnity to silliness to sadness and
onward. Now, we were mostly silent as we shared an orange
and drank from our water bottles, careful to leave enough for
the hot trek down. She'd sweat in patches, I observed, whereas
my t-shirt and shorts were uniformly darkened.

The film of dust that had settled over her pink gave her the
illusion of a tan. She was the palest desert dweller I'd seen, but
seemed blithely unself-conscious of her pallor in this city of
sun worshippers. In contrast, I looked like a native. When,
unconsciously, I reached one brown finger to trace a line of
freckles down her arm, she only smiled.

The trip down was quick, hot, and breathless, as gravity
outstripped the desire for conversation down the steep slope.
I led the way to the shaded water fountain at the base, where,
having finished the last of our bottles, we doused ourselves
before getting into our cars. We both were dry by the time we
got to my house for a quick shower and change of clothes.

She insisted I go first, so I set her up at the kitchen table with the Sunday paper and a frothy mug of juice and seltzer, and hopped into the shower to rinse the dust off. I was in and out in three minutes but took my time toweling off to give her — and me — some time to breathe and assess the morning. I didn't want the exhilaration of the climb to skew my expectations: I'd skinned both knees falling for straight women before, and the memory stung enough to keep me stepping carefully. It wasn't love I wanted now but romance: to indulge in the getting-to-know-you rapture of a burgeoning friendship without drowning in need — to tube the rapids without swallowing the river.

I left a set of towels for her on the edge of the sink, called out to let her know the bathroom was free, and disappeared into my room to change.

She surprised me then, appearing twenty minutes later in a sassy white cotton dress, then turning her back to me with a "Will you?" My hands went hot and clumsy on the zipper. The sprinkling of freckles stopped below her shoulder blades. My stomach stopped at my groin.

The Cinquo de Mayo festivities were still warming up when we arrived at the Buttes in her car, just short of noon. She led the way in, producing two tickets — her treat, her invitation — from a pocket I didn't know she had. Hungry from the climb and from want of a real breakfast, we went first for the food, loading our plates with Indian fry bread, fresh blue-corn tortillas, salsa, beans, guacamole, mesquite-broiled *el pollo*. Balancing a pitcher of water under my plate, I followed her to a ringside table under the slatted roof of the pavilion. We sat and proceeded to feast.

The first of the bands was setting up, and she watched the preparations eagerly while her fingers tucked bite after bite into a mouth as eager as her eyes. She loved dancing as much as I did, and a wider range of music. Half a song and she was out on the concrete, half a plate of food forgotten. We danced together, she danced alone, she danced with any man who asked, charming each for the span of a song or two, but clearly herself charmed by the music. Salsa, jazz, rock, reggae, country swing — her energy never flagged. In between sets and changeovers, we amused each other making up stories about members of the crowd.

She was a terrific flirt. She could have flirted in any language, conjuring response with mirrors, not words: catching the light in the lake of her eyes; tossing it back in a glint of lips, a gleam of shoulder. To be the focus of her attentions was electrifying. My palms and soles hummed.

A troupe of dancers performed, torsos thrusting, feet throbbing hypnotically to the beat of African and Caribbean drums. I knew one of the male dancers through the local food co-op and introduced her to him at her request. As I watched, she looked long at his bare chest and muscled calves, smiling, and touched her lip; I heard him swallow. She led him to the dance floor when the next band struck up, and I watched him whirl and counterstep before her, solar plexus high and forward, his eyes intent on hers.

She was back in three dances.

I told myself again, sternly, not to take her attentions personally. Already, the warning felt like hindsight.

I began to feel drugged, with that split consciousness that says at once, "Whoa, you're losing control," and, "I'm flying, fly me higher." No; yes. Two letters versus three: I could feel the slide of the scales like a ship listing hard starboard as my ribs rose skyward. The mystery here was not what her eyes and fingers and mouth were doing but how powerless I felt to resist them.

I was quiet on the drive to Scottsdale, where we were to meet some friends to attend a gallery opening. She still spilled over with energy, but I had danced hard to shake free of the spell

I'd fallen under and, happy just to feel both feet again, was content for the moment to play appreciative audience.

Our friends couldn't keep the surprise from their faces when they saw us together. It wasn't the fact of our arriving together — we were expected — but her high color and my off-balance grin that surprised them. They knew us from different contexts — her, more or less professionally, through the university; me, socially — and apparently the borders hadn't crossed in their minds.

One — Ricki — took me aside as soon as she gracefully could. "I thought she was straight," she whispered.

"She is," I answered.

Ricki punched me in the arm. "Tomorrow," she said, wagging a finger at me. "I want the dirt."

I laughed and rejoined the entourage.

"Animal Dreams," the show was called. The animals here could not be found in any zoo. Cartoonlike creatures cavorted in big, brilliantly hued paintings; clothed clay beasts prowled the square tops of pedestals; humanlike faces gazed from masks of paint and bone and feathers and teeth and fur. Were these animal dreams of humans or human dreams of animals? I found the work and the theme bizarrely fitting: animal joy, animal hunger, animal mystery.

I quickly left the socializing to the others and wandered off by myself to look at the masks. Peering into the faces, shifting my angle of vision to catch their shifting expressions, I was suddenly struck by the familiarity of the movement. Mirrors, I thought. Here was the artist flirting with the viewer flirting with mystery, power, fear.

One mask stood out from the others. Relatively plain but for a sea green opalescent finish, it featured half-lidded eyeholes and a beaklike nose under a high brow ridge. Small feathers hung at its temples, and the upper lip overhung the lower. Where its wearer's throat would be, a winged vertebra dangled. The unexpected effect was of utter serenity. "Turtlehawk Dreams an Ocean Breathing," the card beside it said.

On impulse, I began experimenting, trying to mirror the mask's expression. How well I succeeded I don't know, but for a moment, before I grew too self-conscious to continue, a feeling rose in me of light, as if I stood in the copper flame of sunset with stars in my head. The pitching sea I'd been riding all day calmed. I wanted to kiss her, and the wanting suffused me with happiness.

Before I could savor the feeling, Ricki snagged me again and dragged me over to view the paintings. Now the work mirrored me: colors of elation, shapes of joy. I grinned and, at a prod from Ricki's elbow, turned. Across the room her eyes flashed "go." A wave washed through me, leaving in joy's stead a feeling cooler, metallic, tall. My hands jumped. My center of balance went south.

"Uh-huh," said Ricki.

◆◆◆◆

We were both quiet as she was driving me home. We had each declined our friends' invitations to go for ice cream, but I, at least, wasn't ready for the day to end. On impulse, as she turned down the road that cut through the desert park near my house, I suggested a moonlight hike. She was more than agreeable.

The small lot near my favorite climb was empty — unusual except on a Sunday night. After we'd parked, she pulled an old quilt from the trunk of her car, and we followed a vague trail up the small red sandstone mountain. Halfway up we spread her quilt, staking out a rounded ledge facing the city to our west, with a shallow cave scooped by hot winds at our backs and a screen of creosote bushes between us and the lot below.

The city lights spread before us; a sea of stars spread over us. Balmy, not even sweater cool, the night air enfolded us in the desert's perfume. Wrapped in this intoxication of sky and dust and creosote and millenia of light, we leaned back, near but not touching, and soaked it all in.

We sat without speaking for a long time, until the erratic flight of a bat caught our attention. We watched it avidly, speculating as to its food, its nesting habits, the reasons for people's fear. We went off on a long tangent then about pocket mice, king snakes, jackrabbits, coyotes.

At this, the moment in the gallery flooded back and I lapsed into silence. What was she remembering?

The quality of the silence had changed. Charged now, the night seemed to be waiting, and we with it.

A moment of laughter was all it took.

The bat came back, with a companion this time, and she made a crack about Dracula's bride. I countered with a slur on Batman and Robin.

"What about Batwoman?" she asked.

"If that's Batwoman," I said, "the other one's Catherine Deneuve."

She frowned at me, confounded, then her eyebrows lifted and her mouth opened and she laughed. "Ah, ha," she said. "And where is Susan Sarandon this evening?"

I nudged her. She nudged me back. We sat for several minutes leaning up against each other, feeling the intersection of our bodies — shoulders, arms, thighs. Finally, I took her hand, brushing the fingertips with my own, tracing, lightly, the grooves of her palm. After a moment, I raised her hand to my lips, kissed each fingertip slowly, touching the faint salt of each with my tongue. I kissed her palm, dragging my lip across the pad at the base of each finger. Where two fingers cleaved, I licked, softly.

I looked at her. Her eyes were closed, her head tipped back and turned slightly away, as if listening for her name. I pressed my face to her palm, closing my eyes, then wrapped my mouth full around her first finger and tugged, drawing the salt from her pores, drawing the blood to her skin, drawing a moan from her opening throat. I met and held her startled gaze as I moved to the next finger, sucking deep, pulling back to take both fingers in. Blood filled my limbs. My tongue swam around and between her fingers. The smell of sun on skin and a hint of sunscreen teased me from the back of her hand. As I breathed it in, I could feel her in me already, how it would be to fill this wanting.

Hooking her thumb under my chin, she pulled my face toward her, hunger and something like danger darkening her eyes. I let her fingers slide from my mouth and waited. Her lips touched mine like smoke from the fire between my thighs, and the center of my chest caught flame. She pressed into me savagely; the world fell away. And came back in a slow kiss made slower by the racing of my pulse. Breathing deep, I savored the silken rim of her sweetly clean mouth, small arc by small arc, welcoming her tongue — the satin underside, the softly nubbled surface — with mine.

How long we kissed I have no idea. Long enough to drown and be resuscitated. We kissed till we reached a clean, clear place in our kissing, and found ourselves wrapped around each other like vines after an April rain, satiated, drunk on fullness. We lolled against each other, laughing. And rested, face against face, breathing the night air.

And then we kissed again, and the hunger rose like a tidal wave from a sea shaken at its floor.

Suddenly four hands weren't enough, and her underwear was in my hand, my pants were to my knees, and she was over me, pinning my wrists to the rock, our arms taut over my head, her face fierce a breath from mine.

Eyes locked on mine, she lowered herself onto me, hot wet scalding my exposed belly. Deliberately, never wavering her gaze, she began to rub, back and forth, up and down, down and around. I was drowning in sensation. Juices flowed from me like hot tears. Feeling her gyrations beginning to center on my bush, I stretched myself longer — longer to stretch her longer, to feel the length of her body rolling against mine.

She wriggled lower, pulling my wrists down to my shoulders, her mouth at my chest seeking skin but finding shirt. She sat up, releasing my arms, to concentrate instead on her movements. My hands found her under her dress and gripped, slipping over the slick muscles of her thighs and buttocks as she rode me. Her hands gripped my ribs, then my thighs as she leaned back, pressing up on me. My pelvis and neck arched hard as I angled for fuller contact. I closed my eyes to focus on the center of our juncture.

We were like two oppositely charged wires, the voltage jumping in each with each roll of our hips, the ends brushing closer and closer, tantalizingly close to contact. Small sounds fluttered from her throat; my breath soughed through narrowed lips. Heat engulfed my pubis as my whole being strained toward her. The ends of the wires moved closer and closer, millimeters apart now, current leaping the liquid between them.

And then they touched. A deep shudder shook us both. A wave of liquid heat swept the insides of my legs and rolled from my feet, and the backlash rippled audibly through my chest and neck. She remained arched back, breathing long, loose breaths like sighs.

Kicking my ankles finally free of my pants and unbuttoning my shirt with one hand, I stretched the other behind her and unzipped what I had zipped that morning. Easing the dress from her shoulders, then over her head, I pulled her to me. Breast to breast, mouth to liquid mouth, we steeped in our mingled sweat.

We ended up on our sides, murmuring together forehead to forehead, stroking the length of each other's body, for a long spell. Then the sound of tires on blacktop and a sweep of headlights below us swung me upright. Through the web of creosote I watched a lone car pass through the park.

When I turned back, she was smiling, her body a feast of cream in the starlight. Feeling a purr begin in my chest, I bent to the cream, lapping the bowl of her belly and ribs with long sweeps as she drew her fingers through my hair. I worked my way slowly up to her breasts, nuzzling and lapping each nipple till it stood, then painting broad wet circles around the near nipple with my tongue. Eyes closed, she kneaded the small of my back with one hand, tracing my face with the other. I twined one fingertip in her damp pubic curls, then shifted to straddle one leg.

Cupping in my hand the breast I'd been licking, I leaned over her and took into my mouth as much as I could of the other. I sucked slowly with my whole mouth, alternately flicking the round berry with the tip of my tongue. Her hands tangled in my hair, urging me to her. The other berry I brushed with my thumb till I could feel her begin to undulate beneath me.

Her grip on my head tightened, and when I raised my head to look at her, she seized me to her, mouth open, devouring mine, all teeth and jaw and tongue and need. She engulfed my chin, scraping my neck with her teeth, sliding her hot mouth over my larynx. I broke away, startled, stiff-arming the rock we lay on to hold myself above her. We stared at each other.

My arms bent. I devoured back, flattening myself against her as she gripped my buttocks and thrust her thigh between my legs. I bucked against her, smearing her thigh with my juices. Our nipples chafed together. I ground my hip into her, and myself against hers.

My fingers found her vagina and I thrust two in to the knuckle. She bucked and shuddered and broke from my mouth with a cry. I rolled to her side. Her hips began to rock and rotate; her hands clutched at the quilt. Whimpering gasps sprang from her chest. I began sliding my fingers in and out with a long twisting motion. Her vagina ballooned. My fingertips circled her cervix. Her cervix pushed back.

My thumb on her clit, fingers pressing upward against the washboard inside, I began moving my whole arm in circles, slowly at first, faster as her hips responded as if with a mind of their own. Knees bent, her feet pressed into the rock, she bore down on me, hips in the air jerking up and down, side to side, circling with me and against me. I closed my eyes and labored to stay with her.

My own body was on the verge of orgasm, my genitals so engorged I could have come at a touch. My skin sang; a howl leapt within my throat. I held my thighs tightly closed.

Her cries filled my chest, high grunting moans that punctuated her quickening thrusts. A quick inbreath and suddenly she went silent, her hips suspended in motion. A low cry began in her belly then, rising in pitch and volume as her vagina convulsed around my fingers and her hips jerked and dropped and her hands seized my shoulders and held on.

We lay, spent, for several minutes. Then, my fingers still in her, I leaned over to taste her. She shivered. I knelt carefully between her legs and parted her hairs with my other hand. She groaned and reached for my head, then fell back. Stretching my legs out behind me, I folded my arm under my chest and bellied up, touched my lips to those lips, and exhaled hotly. She sighed. I touched my tongue to the underside of her clit. Her breath caught, and resumed. Easing my fingers halfway out, I licked them, savoring the heady fragrance on my tongue. And continued my slow lick up to rub my nose in her wet curls.

She swept her feet up my sides, gripping my head a moment, then rested them on my shoulder blades, her knees flung wide.

I lapped the spill of cream from the satin grooves either side of her clitoris. Then, gently, slowly, as I enfolded her clit in my lips, I began wiggling my fingers alternately back and forth inside her. I made my tongue as soft and flat as possible, tracing small, gentle circles against her. When I felt that bud swell I began sucking softly and running my tongue up again and again from her innermost lips.

I let my fingers slip from her and my tongue take their place. A low "oh" escaped her, and she pressed against me, tightening her vagina as I reached deeply in, kissing me back as thoroughly as she had with her mouth.

I drank her in and in.

Slick-faced, I returned at last to her clit, breathing on it softly, circling it with the tip of my tongue. Her hips echoed the motion almost imperceptibly. I continued the circles, slowly increasing my pressure as her circles became more pronounced. Occasionally I let my tongue flicker across her, resuming the circling as she would stop hers and begin to moan. Finally, she began to squirm against my mouth with a low whimper.

I began flicking her clit in earnest and slipped my fingers back into her to resume my back-and-forth motion. She began rocking up and down, her whole body now, and her whimper took on the same quick rhythm.

With my free hand I pressed her mound, pushing the skin back to expose her further. My flicking became a vibration, a thrum humming all through me, electrifying my fingertips, toes, clit. I felt as though I were licking myself, each flicker of tongue on her bringing me closer to combustion. But it was her I wanted, on me and in me. The force of my wanting narrowed to twin points of flame on the tips of my tongue and clitoris.

Her feet clutching my ribs urged me on. Faster and faster came her staccato song; faster and faster came my answer. Then, as her rocking became a pulse and the hum became a roar, she jerked — almost sitting up — and jerked, jerked, jerked, jerked, each spasm smaller, subsiding like a basketball's dribble to a state of rest.

When her walls had stopped fluttering and our breathing had slowed to normal and the evaporation of sweat was at last beginning to chill our skin, I eased my fingers from her and climbed up to her head. She looked at me. "Lover," she said.

I grinned hugely and flopped on my back next to her, one hand rubbing my still-wet belly.

She nuzzled her way into my armpit, and I wrapped her in skin.

I was in some other space, breathing night, lulled by star-song, when I became conscious of something sharp brushing my nipple. I opened my eyes to find her teasing her fingernails across my breast. Seeing me looking, she sat up.

She looked at me then, at my body, running her hands along my skin as though her fingertips held another set of eyes. I wondered if she'd ever really looked at another woman's body before. She kept returning to my breasts, cupping their curve in her palms, rolling my pursed nipples under her thumbs, bending finally to touch her tongue to one. She closed her lips around it carefully, exploring its tip with her tongue, pressing into my breast when I drew a quick breath and held it. Heat was beginning again its spread from my center.

She laid her face against my belly for a moment, turning her head back and forth to feel the smoothness against each cheek. My ribs began to prickle; my breath, to quicken.

I felt a finger teasing my bush hairs and stifled a moan — a moan she dragged from me in the next moment, her fingernails leaving four hot trails down the inside of each thigh. I started to sit up; she pressed me back into the rock.

She pushed my legs open wider and knelt between them. I curved around to watch her.

As she leaned in to look, I could feel my juices begin their slow cascade from my vagina. Sure enough, a touch and she held up a finger: on its tip a dollop of cream. Watching me carefully, she painted her mouth with it. She licked. She smiled. My insides flipped. I closed my eyes as desire flooded my forearms and thighs.

At the touch of her thumb pulling back the hood of my clit, I looked again. She was peering closely through the dim light into my spread lips. Her lips pursed. She blew across me. My vagina contracted, releasing another daub. She touched me again and painted the smooth wet along my ribs.

She seemed to make a decision then and surprised me by moving to my side. She bent to kiss me — a short, sweet kiss, in the middle of which something like fire — her fingertip — seared the underside of my clit. A jolt shot through me.

She moved her mouth to my breast again, tonguing and sucking and rubbing her whole face over me. That single point of heat stayed on my clitoris, even as I began to writhe under the intensity.

She stayed with me, breaking her touch only to dip again into the river of my juices. Was her finger moving, was I moving against her, was this heat pure energy and not friction at all?

I only knew that my skin was raging, that I wanted her wrapping me like a fresh dressing on a burn. Or was it a match I wanted, ready to immolate myself on her pyre? I heaved my hips at that point of fire, bracing my arms and shoulders against the rock like a sacrifice.

All my consciousness came to exist in that single point of contact as that hot coal grew hotter. All awareness of my body vanished, though I continued to thrash, that incendiary urge driving me toward combustion. But the higher the heat climbed, the higher my threshold for heat seemed to rise. Thrash as I might, I could come no closer to flame.

Finally, I no longer knew whether I was chasing flame or fleeing it. A groan tore my throat.

She dipped again but this time came back above my clit, stroking the stiff root above the hood. Something in me melted. My body came back. I could feel her length stretched along my leg now, her head resting on my hip, my hands — one lost in her hair, the other pressing my own mound — the pleasure flowing from my center with each rub of my root. A long "aaahhh" rolled from my chest. I rode the pleasure as if floating in a tropical sea, saturated with sun and lazy with longing answered. Dipping and bobbing, I let the swells lift me like breath, deliver me like breath. Closer and closer to sky I rode, basking in the billowing flow till the ocean rose in me and flung its swollen waters on my shore.

I lowed.

She slipped over my chest to cover me like a wave. My mouth found hers and submerged. All was water. We twined together like anemones on the sea floor, wet on wet every-where, swimming in each other, around each other, our mouths and limbs and fingers everywhere at once. Turning, diving, flipping, and sliding in an underwater dance, we skimmed bottom. We sang sea. We came up for air to find ourselves mirroring each other, sitting mouth to mouth, breasts to breasts, legs scissored around each other, one over, one under, our cunts open and joined.

That night I would dream of ocean, dream an ocean breathing.

Past lives

◆◆◆◆   *Jane Futcher*

S he lives in a suburb, and she is there now in her ranch
house overlooking the coast oaks and hayfields beyond. She walks among her appliances — microwave, washer
and dryer, Cuisinart, remote-control TV — barefoot and naked,
except for her red jockey shorts.

"How many red jockey shorts do you own?" I ask.

"I don't know. Maybe five." Morgan sees my smile. "The
blood doesn't show as much with red undies." Her periods are
war zones. Blood bursts and spills and gushes forth from her
womb; her bandages must be changed often.

She is in her house now, playing back the twenty-two
phone messages that came while we sat in the warm, steamy
baths of Calistoga. There are messages from her seventeen-
year-old daughter, who is staying the night in San Francisco;
from her nineteen-year-old in New Mexico, who will marry a
soldier in December; from her ex-husband in Berkeley, looking for the seventeen-year-old; from her mother with news of
a close-out sale; from her business partner, who wonders
who's on back-up; from her high school friend Elise, with
whom she fell in love two years ago.

◆◆◆◆

We escape to Calistoga, wandering from bed to the hot pools and back to the bed, where she presses me to the mattress with the same strong arms that catch babies from the wombs of writhing mothers.

Her eyes are blue like a cat's, unblinking, and lined with dark lashes, top and bottom. I stare at her eyes till the clock melts, locked in her safe, unwavering gaze. She sees the black carp floating motionless in my heart, but she does not fear their accusations — that I sucked my father's cock and opened my small child thighs to my mother's painted fingernails.

I crawl up the calm of her legs to her white breasts, to her mane, wild and gold. Her fingers wind through my hair; she tugs my head to her lips. I am one of her garden plants, her blue lobelia, her bleeding heart.

"Make me pregnant," I whisper. She tugs tighter and reaches for my thighs.

"I want your baby," I say, wrapping my legs around her waist.

She laughs. "You're going to have to raise it. I've had two already. That's enough."

"I'll raise her," I say, "and she will be wild and freckled and blue-eyed like you."

Her tongue touches my lips. "I love you," she says. "I love you." Her lavender-pink lips open mine. She rocks me, moves up and down me, enters and reenters me. I want to marry her shoulders, her lungs, her deep, calm belly.

"Bite my nipples," she whispers in my ear.

I suck her erect, pink breasts.

"Harder," she says.

I cannot bite harder. "I'm afraid I'll hurt you," I say.

"Hurt me," she says. "Hurt me a little."

Instead, I kiss the smooth skin between her neck and chest. I am her child now, sibling of the seventeen-year-old who stretches languidly in front of the TV, renting videos, waiting for her life to begin. I have never met my other sibling, who lives in New Mexico studying herbs.

They are exotic, these women, in their California ranch house, with their Magic Genie garage door and their mystical appliances. Sometimes, when their mother holds me, she hums a song that has no tune; I drift back centuries, to the desert, to ancient fires, to a witch stirring remedies in a cauldron beneath the midsummer sun.

"My bowels freeze up around you," I tell her.

She looks at me, her fingers still inside me.

"You can't poo?" *Poo* seems an odd word for a sorceress to use.

I nod. "I'm embarrassed to make smells and gassy sounds around you. My bowels lock."

She stares at the ceiling. "My bowels haven't moved today either," she says. I am surprised. She is a natural woman. I thought her bowels would always move. Knowing this, she is my friend, and sister. She is as weak as I am.

When she drives her car fast on the freeway, weaving through traffic, cruising for cops in the rearview mirror, she is my husband. When she hauls my massage table to the car as if it were light, she is my husband. She is my wife when she chops garlic and zucchini and broccoli and scallions and cooks them on the flame, quietly, creating a taste beyond heaven. She is my wife when I lie on top of her, and her legs open beneath my womb; she is soft and bleats like a lamb.

"I want to fuck you," I say to her gaze.

She studies me a moment more and opens her legs. "Go ahead."

"I want to lick you first, then fuck you," I say.

"Please," she says. "Do it." She holds her ankles in her hands so that I can find her pink, soft places. I smell her pussy, fresh, like the sweetgrass baskets the gypsies sold us in the summers. She rises and lifts to the slow, hard circles of my tongue. Her sounds are soft, excited; she is hungry. I place her fingers on her clit so she can spur the visions and thorns of pleasure. Her cries build to a low wail. "My darling," I whisper, as she writhes. "My wife," I moan, as she comes.

◆◆◆◆

In the motel, our periods arrive at the same exact moment — the same red blood on the same white toilet paper. We wake that night with blood and cramps and pain. We laugh and whisper and take Advil until four a.m.

"I'll hypnotize you back to sleep," I say finally, and count slowly down from ten, down deeper, down the staircase into the safe, dark earth. Her eyes close, her limbs twitch, her breath deepens, and she is gone. I lie next to her, hot and sexy and awake. Her snores startle, then arouse me. Her maleness excites me.

"I am not male," she says. "I am all female. Varieties of female. A female who drives fast, a female who snores, a female who lifts heavy things." I fall asleep, wet and aching, my head against her shoulder.

I sleep. I dream. I dream I am with Ellie, my ex-lover, in the bathroom. We lie by the bathtub, naked. Ellie has a penis and is on top of me, fucking me. It feels like swimming, like the gods sliding in and out of me; her breasts slurp against mine as she thrusts and moans. Her sweat drips into my mouth. She is coming, I am coming. I am afraid that her teenage sons will discover us.

"They're in college," she whispers. "They're away." She licks my breasts and climbs inside me.

"What about Cassandra?" Cassandra is her lover.

"She's at work." Ellie's dick is about to explode. I am worried about Morgan. What will I say to her? I have promised I will tell her if there is someone else, and here I am, fucking Ellie, who is hard with desire.

"Hello?" The door opens in the dream; a bright light shatters our eyes. Cassandra is standing over us, dark and slender and surprised. She is Burmese and speaks with a crisp British accent. "I'm sorry," she says, when she sees us. She lowers her eyes.

Ellie withdraws her penis and stands up. "We were just looking for Tampax," she says cheerfully. We stare down at our naked bodies; fingerprints of menstrual blood are smeared across our bellies.

Cassandra looks away. "I'll forget what I saw," she says, and closes the door quietly.

I am trembling. "I don't understand. She's not mad? Why isn't she..."

"She's fine." Ellie cocks her head. "She doesn't see it. She doesn't mind."

But Morgan will mind. How will I explain my fucking Ellie?

I wake up, heart thudding. Morgan is cradling me in her arms. My cheek still rests on her shoulder. I have not betrayed her. I fall back to sleep.

I am still asleep when I enter the living room of the house in Baltimore where I grew up. My dead mother has come to visit in her nightgown; she is alive but frail. Her hair is gray and falling out from chemotherapy.

"Mom, hello," I say. "Is it really you?" I am crying with pleasure.

She nods and smiles.

I hug her. I hold her fragile body. "I've missed you so much."

"Yes," she says. "But I'm here now."

I hold her bony hand. It is still warm. I hope she will not notice that my father has changed the living room around. On the mahogany coffee table he has placed a photo of a woman with large breasts in a bikini; his arm is around her waist.

"Where do you go?" I ask. "What is it like to be dead? Where will you go next?"

She smiles sadly. "I don't know."

"Can I visit you? Will you come back?" I am crying hard now. "Mom, don't leave yet. Please, stay."

I wake up. I am holding Morgan. I hug her tightly.

After the pools, we drive south, back to Morgan's house, which is painted red.

"I want to see a picture of you as a hippie," I say, as she unpacks. Morgan left home at seventeen to take acid and live in Haight-Ashbury. She was a real hippie, right out of *Life* magazine, living in a commune, wearing flowers in her hair, hitchhiking in vans and smoking pot.

She finds several albums and shows me a shot of herself laughing, in a ponytail, wearing a peasant dress, braless, and walking barefoot in a stream. I want to see more, so I take the albums to the bedroom and lie down. I study her past. There are hundreds of photographs of people I don't know, of a woman I don't know. I am intrigued.

"Ah," she says, as my eyes lock on a black-and-white photograph. "My wedding." She wears a white dress and white pants and a garland of flowers on her head; her eyes closed, she sits in a circle, meditating. A bearded man is cross-legged next to her. My heart lunges. I do not want to see this. I do not want to see her getting married. I know it was twenty years ago; it is only fiction now, a memory, but I am jealous, and I do not want to see it. Still, I cannot stop. I touch the photograph, reach back into time, long to sit down next to Morgan and marry her myself.

I cannot think what to say. I mustn't look anymore, but I continue turning the pages. The blood drains from my face with each new image. My eyes stick again, this time to a close-up of Morgan, forehead taut, teeth clenched, neck muscles bulging, eyes closed.

"Allie's birth," she laughs. I inhale. Allie is her older daughter. In the next picture, she is naked; her breasts are engorged and beautiful; her knees are spread wide; a woman leans over her. A dark, wet head is poking out of her vagina. The camera is so close you can see the hairs on Morgan's legs — only her name is not Morgan, it is Kirn Kaura — and she is wearing socks. Naked except for socks. I turn away, turn back. In the last photo of the sequence, she is smiling weakly, exhausted and pale, touching the cheek of the bearded man with unspeakable tenderness.

I want to be that man she is touching. I want to be the father of her baby. Close the book, I tell myself. Don't look anymore. But I turn back. Morgan/Kirn Kaura is pregnant again. She is wearing a white turban and she walks with the erect posture of a goddess. Her husband is also in white, in a turban. He is the chief yogi and she is his wife and a yogini herself. I see men and women and babies everywhere. I am an alien. I have left my body, am wandering among the dead. I see other men she loved. I see women. I watch her daughters growing breasts. Morgan is telling me about the people in the pictures — "That is Sim Singh, who ran the ashram in New Mexico. That is Maysoon in the ashram in L.A. Those are my girls with Yogi Mishra."

There are so many men, so many children, so many wives that I am not listening. I am thinking of the psychiatrist in Philadelphia who told me it was wrong for my father to examine me, even if he was a doctor. I am remembering New York — Eighth Avenue — wall to wall with lesbians in a gay pride march. I am living with Maggie in Greenwich Village, drinking cappucino at Bleeker People, where so many of our gay friends worked. I am remembering the night in Boston when I told my parents I was a lesbian. My father stared into the fire; my mother cried, asked if I'd ever have children, and never again mentioned the subject. I am desperate, alone, afraid to touch or be touched; the very thought of having a child fills me with terror. I am an outlaw, outside the mainstream, even outside the outlaws.

I want to be touched by the woman who has just given birth to my child.

"Lucy?" Morgan moves closer. "What's wrong?"

I can't talk. I am ashamed and angry and guilty. "Nothing," I say.

Morgan pushes the books away, pulls me next to her. "I love you," she whispers. Her touch is gentle and reassuring. I soften. I feel desire in my legs, waves of motion in my belly. She unbuttons my jeans and pulls them slowly down over my knees. She spreads me open and kisses my thighs. "I love you," she says again, her eyes looking up and over the hair of my crotch toward the white skin of my breasts. Her tongue laps me, slides over me. I am aroused. She is no longer Morgan. She is Kirn Kaura, a woman in a white turban, a goddess, a mystic married to a man from Brooklyn with a seven-syllable Sanskrit name. She is a man now, with a black beard and a speculum; she is her wide-lipped actress daughter. She is my father and his tongue, she is my mother opening my legs. I am stoned on LSD, lying on a high plain in New Mexico, eating tofu and brown rice and mushrooms.

Morgan stops. "Lucy? What's wrong?"

"Nothing," I say. I cannot tell her.

"Are you sure?"

"Can you hold me?" I whisper finally. "Can you come up here and hold me?"

She covers me with the sheet and rocks me in her arms. We lie in silence. My eyes are closed. I am frozen.

"Talk to me," she says. "What's wrong?"

"I don't know."

She touches my eyelids with her fingertips. "Is it so bad?"

I shake my head. "It's bad," I say.

"What is?"

"How I feel."

Her eyes puzzle over me. "What do you feel?"

I inhale. I want to hide. I make myself say it. I have promised Morgan the truth. "I am jealous of your past."

"Was it the pictures?" she asks softly.

I nod, ashamed. "I am jealous of your husband and your children and your life. I can't get the ashram and the turbans and the yogis out of my mind. My father and mother are fucking me. Your husband is fucking me. You are all of them, and I feel like dying."

"Sweetheart," she says. "Hold me tighter."

"Everything seems hopeless," I say. "We're so different."

She is quiet, but she is not angry. I can feel her grounding herself, preparing for further pain, sending her taproot down into the earth. "Sweetheart, I left my husband and the ashram a long time ago. I left them because I didn't belong anymore. Now is now. Now I'm here with you. No one else is here. No men, no parents. Just me. I love you. I love you more than I've ever loved anyone."

More than I've ever loved anyone. I hear the words, but I cannot feel them. I am too lost in the past — in my fantasy of her past, in the cruelty of my own past.

She strokes my hair. "Those people, those events have made us both who we are. I love your past — it has made you the person you are today. Our pasts have led us to each other. We don't need to be afraid. You know?"

I blink. I blink away the yogis and the bearded men and my parents. "You are very generous," I whisper. "I wish I were as generous as you."

"I'm not so generous. I'd feel the same way looking at your photos. But we're fine. We're okay. You're here. I'm here. We love each other. We're alive. We're healthy. Is it really so tragic?"

"I'm tragic," I say with a tiny smile.

"Perhaps I should tickle you." Her hands reach for my armpits.

"No, don't." But she is tickling me, mounting me, wrestling me down with the arms that catch babies as they drop from wombs.

"Freckle, flower, friend," I say, and strangely, with the words, the love returns, the pictures dissolve. Here, finally, is Morgan, with blue eyes and freckled cheekbones; strong and wise, like a cat. The others are gone, as her fingertips tighten on my breasts, as she heaves inside me, as her mouth opens to mine. There is only one image left now — a hippie, long-haired and blonde, tan and shirtless, pressed into jeans, hand in my pants, unbuttoning my blouse. I come to her coming. After that, she holds me tight.

A true story (Whether you believe it or not)

◆◆◆◆   *Lesléa Newman*

This is a true story, and it happened to me, Zoey B. Jackson, on the twelfth of May, whether you believe it or not. And to tell you the truth, it's kinda hard for me to believe it myself. It's the sorta thing someone would make up to impress a girl they just met at a party or something, but believe me, I could never make this up. I could never even imagine such a thing happening and least of all happening to me, but it did, sure as I'm standing here telling about it.

Well, there I was, in the Famous Deli, which isn't famous for much, except maybe its slow service, waiting for Larry, the kid behind the counter, to make me two BLTs on rye. I was just standing there minding my own business, studying the different cheeses in the deli case and wondering how they make one cheese taste different from the next and why they bother. I mean cheese is cheese as far as I can tell. Cheddar, Muenster, Monterey Jack — do they use different kinds of cows for different kinds of cheeses or what?

I guess my mind was a little fuzzy, sort of like a TV that's outa focus. I had just spent two hours trying to get a cat down out of a tree and I wasn't in the greatest mood of my life. When

I joined the fire department two years ago, cats stuck up in trees wasn't exactly what I had in mind. I wanted to be a fireman ever since I was a little girl, only my mama said I couldn't — little girls don't grow up to be firemen. Or policemen or businessmen or garbagemen or any other kind of men at all.

But I didn't care what my mama said. I usta dream about riding in a fire truck with the lights flashing and the sirens screaming, wearing a big red hat and racing through town with a black-and-white dog wagging its tail on the back. I got a piggy bank shaped like a fire truck for my birthday once, and I used to sleep with the thing. Still have it too.

So when I turned forty, two years ago, I decided to come work for the FD as a present to myself. I didn't want no fame or glory or nothing, but I did have visions of myself on the front page of the *Tri-Town Tribune* all dirty and sweaty, having worked all night putting out a fire and saving a couple of lives. I was in the paper actually, but not for any heroic deeds or nothing, but because of my size. I don't know whether it's something to be proud about or something to be ashamed about, but I'm the smallest person in the history of the whole state to ever join the fire department, and only the second woman. Probably the first lesbian too, but you know they didn't put that in the paper. I'm just about five feet tall when I ain't slouching, and I weigh about a hundred pounds soaking wet, but it's all solid muscle. I can whip that hose around like nobody's business when I have to.

But that night I didn't have to do nothing fancy. I mean whose idea was it to call the fire department to get a cat down out of a tree anyway? People watch too many cartoons, that's what I think. When we got there, we meaning me and Al, old Mrs. Lawrence was standing under that tree crying and carrying on like it was her husband or one of her kids up there instead of her stupid old cat, Matilda. She had Matilda's dish out there full of food, and all her favorite toys — a whiffle ball, a sock full of catnip, and a tangle of yarn. She was practically on her knees begging that animal to please, *please* come on down. Mrs. Lawrence was promising her all sorts of things — she'd feed Matilda fresh fish and sour cream every day, and she'd let her sleep in bed with her, and she wouldn't yell anymore when Matilda sharpened her claws on the living room furniture, if only Matilda would *get down*. I guess old Matilda had been up there for most of the day yowling, and by this time it was ten at night and the neighbors were trying to get some sleep. Half of them were out in Mrs. Lawrence's yard in their PJs trying to figure out what to do. It was probably the most exciting thing that had happened in that part of town in about ten years.

So me and Al made a big show of getting the ladder out and climbing up there and getting Matilda down. Ornery thing she was too — sunk her claws deep into that branch, fluffed out her tail till it was fat as a coon's, and hissed at Al fiercer than a rattlesnake. He finally grabbed her, getting his face scratched in the process, tucked her under his arm, and climbed down the ladder with everybody cheering except poor Mrs. Lawrence, who couldn't even bring herself to look.

Once Matilda was safe in Mrs. Lawrence's arms, everyone went back home to bed, and me and Al got into the fire truck to come back to the fire station and make out a report. We stopped at the deli first though, for something to eat, like we usually do. For some reason, most foods taste better at midnight than they do in the middle of the day, you know what I mean? We usually get sandwiches, sometimes coffee and a piece of pie. Al likes strawberry; I go for lemon meringue or banana cream.

So Al was sitting in the truck outside waiting, and I was standing by the counter inside waiting, and I was beginning to think Larry was standing behind the counter waiting too, for the bacon to be delivered maybe, or for the pig to grow old enough to be slaughtered or something, it was taking so goddamn long, but then in walked this woman and all of a sudden I didn't care if those sandwiches didn't get made till half past next July.

She sure was pretty. More than pretty. Gorgeous. A real looker. Awesome, like the kids on Mrs. Lawrence's block would say. I knew she was a stranger around here, 'cause I know every woman in this town — those who do, those who don't, and those who might. This one would, I was sure of it.

She was wearing jeans that fit her just right — tight enough to give you a good idea of what was under 'em, but loose enough to keep you guessing just a little bit. She had on this red shirt that was cut straight across the shoulders so that her collarbone was peeking out a little bit and I could just see the edge of her bra strap, which was black and lacy. She had on these little red shoes that damn near broke my heart and a mess of silver bracelets on her right arm that made a heck of a noise sliding down her wrist and crashing into each other when she reached into her purse for her wallet. There musta been fifty of 'em or more. Her pocketbook was red too and so were her nails and so was her lipstick. Not too red though. Not cheap red or flashy red. There's red and there's *red*, you know what I mean, and this red looked real good. She had silver hoops in her ears, to match her bracelets maybe, and she was a big woman, which suited me fine. I like my women big, you know, like those old painters like Renoir usta paint. None of this Twiggy stuff for me. I like a woman you can hold onto. A woman you're not afraid you're gonna break if you squeeze too tight. A woman with a little meat on her bones.

Well, I took all of this in in about two seconds flat and then I looked away, 'cause I didn't want her to think I was being impolite or nothing. I know my manners and my mama taught me it's real rude to stare. But I just couldn't help it, and before I knew it I found myself looking at her again. Mind your manners, I said to my eyeballs, but they just wouldn't. I watched her unzip this little blue change purse she had and take out two quarters for a soda and then before I could say boo she was looking right back at me with her deep brown eyes, the color of a Hershey's Special Dark, which happens to be my favorite candy bar. And she smiled at me slow, a real sexy smile like she knew she was looking good and I knew she was looking good and she knew that I knew that she was looking good and that made her look even better.

"Hey, Zoey, here's your chow."

Wouldn't you know it? Just when things were starting to get interesting, Larry got my order done. I took my sandwiches, paid for 'em, and would've tipped my hat, but I'd left it out in the truck with Al. I just kinda nodded my head at her, or made some such gesture that was meant to be gallant but probably looked foolish instead. I walked past her, catching a whiff of perfume that almost made me dizzy, and left the deli with another vision to add to my fantasy life, which is about the most exciting action there is around here for an old bulldyke like me. I dunno why I stay in this town, giving all the PTA ladies something to gossip about. I could tell them a thing or two myself, but that's another story.

Well, we weren't back in the firehouse for more than ten minutes when the phone rings. I let Al get it, since my mouth was full of sandwich and he had downed his in about three seconds flat.

"It's for you," Al said, and I don't know who was more surprised, him or me. I never get calls at work. We're not supposed to tie up the phone in case there's a fire or another cat stuck up in a goddamn tree or something, and anyway, I keep my personal life, what little there's left of it anyway, pretty much of a secret, though it's crystal clear I'm as queer as a three-dollar bill even if I don't wear lavender on Thursdays. I think it was the first phone call I'd gotten in the whole two years I'd worked there. I wiped the mayo off my chin with the back of my sleeve, took the phone, and spoke in my most official-sounding voice.

"Hello?"

"Hello. Is this Zoey?"

I knew it was her. I couldn't believe it, yet I wasn't surprised. A little startled, a little shook up, even shocked maybe, but not surprised. She sounded like she looked. Good. Sassy. Sure of herself. And hot.

"Yeah, this is me." God, what a dumb thing to say.

"My name is Natalie, and I was just in the deli a little while ago. I don't know if you noticed me or not" (she had to be kidding), "but I noticed you and I was wondering if you'd like to go out and have a cup of coffee with me sometime?"

How about right this second, I wanted to say, but I didn't. Get a grip, Zoey old girl, I said to myself. Don't rush into anything now.

"Uh, sure, yeah, that'd be great," I said, sounding about thirteen years old.

"How about tomorrow then, around four?"

"Sure," I said, "you know where Freddy's is?" Freddy's is the only place in town that sells a decent cup of coffee and doesn't have a million high school kids throwing spitballs at each other in the middle of the afternoon. It's not sleazy or anything, it's a little out of town, and it's not far from my place as a matter of fact. I explained to her how to get there and then there wasn't much left to say.

"See you tomorrow, Sugar," she said, and I swear I could feel her tongue licking the inside of my ear right through that telephone.

I hardly slept at all that night, I tell you. I was more than a little curious and more than a lot flattered, and hell, I figured that any woman with that much sass deserved at least an hour of my time, and hopefully more. I wondered where she had come from and what she was doing out there by herself all spruced up like that in the middle of the night. But to tell you the truth, I didn't really care. I was just glad she was where she was when she was, and that I was there too.

I tossed and turned, too full of BLT and lust to sleep, but I musta dozed off sometime, 'cause the next thing I knew it was ten o'clock and the sun was coming in through the windows, heating up my eyes like they was two eggs cooking on a grill. My bedroom is tiny — one wall is mostly windows and the bed takes up almost the whole room. I don't mind though, in fact I kinda like it like that. Feels sort of like a nest, though why I have a double bed at this point is beyond me. Ain't nobody been in it since Sally left, over two years ago. Hard to believe it's been two years already. Time sure does fly, I guess. But it musta been, 'cause she left right before I turned forty, right before I signed up at the fire department. That's one of the reasons I did it — with Sally gone there was this empty space in my life, this aching in my belly I didn't know how to fill, and I just couldn't face all those awful lonely nights by myself. So now I sit in the firehouse two, sometimes three, nights a week, playing poker with Al.

I sure didn't wanna be thinking about Sally this morning, so I got up, plugged in the coffee pot, and went into the jane to splash some cold water on my face. "Looking good, old girl," I said to myself in the mirror over the sink, which I noticed was speckled with old toothpaste. "Who says Zoey B. is over the hill, huh? Women are still beating down your door, old gal." I winked at my reflection — I am a pretty good winker if I do say so myself and I can also raise one eyebrow at a time — it's not as hard as it looks if you practice. I looked at myself and wondered what Natalie — God, even her name was sexy — had seen last night standing in the deli that made her call. Your basic brown eyes, two of 'em natch, a straight nose, average lips, nothing special.

Maybe it was the uniform. Some girls really go in for that sorta thing. Or maybe it was the gray hair at the temples, makes me look kinda distinguished. Some girls like older women. I wondered how old Natalie was. And if she did this sort of thing often. Maybe her buddies, whoever they were, had put her up to it. Maybe a whole gang would be waiting at Freddy's to laugh their heads off at the old bulldyke that'd been taken in by the first pretty face that's shown up in this pint-sized town since 1959. Or worse, maybe there'd be some guys waiting with chains and billy clubs ready to kick ass. Like I said, it's no secret who I am and it's no secret that some folks in this town don't exactly like it either. That was really hard on Sally, one of the reasons she left, I think. Nothing ugly's ever happened, but we were always thinking it might. Sally took herself to San Francisco, where she says the streets are paved with queers and she can even hold hands with her new girlfriend all over town and nobody bats an eye. Not even the cops, 'cause even most of the goddamn cops are queer themselves. That's something I'd sure like to see, I tell ya.

Well, I drank my coffee and messed around most of the day, cleaning up the house and doing chores. My place is small, just the bedroom, the kitchen, the living room, and a small spare room where I keep all my junk — my tools and papers and stuff. Usta be Sally's room for painting — that's what she does is paint — watercolors mostly. She even had a show of 'em in San Francisco, sent me a postcard all about it.

Well, by three o'clock I started getting nervous. First of all, what the heck was I gonna wear? Not that I had much choice. It was either jeans or jeans. Jeans with a ripped knee, jeans speckled with white paint, or jeans with two belt loops missing. I could wear my black chinos, but that'd look awful funny, me being so dressed up in the middle of the day. I put on the jeans with the belt loops missing and a white shirt I thought about ironing and my sneaks. By the time I'd finished fussing with my hair, which is only about two inches long and not all that much to fuss about, it was time to get my ass out the door. I sure didn't wanna be late — something told me Natalie wasn't the kinda woman who liked to be kept waiting.

It only took me ten minutes to walk to Freddy's. I got there at four o'clock on the nose and she wasn't there. Well, fine, I told myself. I don't care. Ain't the first time Zoey B.'s been stood up, not the first time she's looked like an old fool. I sat myself down in a booth toward the back, ordered myself a cup of coffee, and looked at my watch. Four-oh-four. Ah well, I thought, ripping open a packet of sugar and dumping it into my cup. I knew it was too good to be true. These things don't really happen. Not in real life anyway.

At exactly ten after four, the door to Freddy's swung, and I mean swung, open and in waltzed Natalie like she owned the whole goddamn place. She was looking so good I almost dove straight into my coffee. I held onto that cup for dear life as she stuck her hands on her hips and looked around like she had all the time in the world. When she spotted me, a slow smile crept across her face that said, I knew you'd be waiting for me. I smiled too, thinking to myself, fool, of course she'd be late. She didn't just wanna meet me here. She wanted to make an *entrance*.

I watched Natalie walk across Freddy's slowly, giving me plenty of time to admire her as she weaved her butt in and out of tables and chairs on her way to where I was sitting. She was wearing this white blousy thing with a belt at her waist, and these pink pants that had little black designs all over 'em that reminded me of slanty tic-tac-toe boards. She had on little pink shoes that knocked me out, round pink earrings that looked like buttons, and a shiny black purse. It's those little things that separate the butches from the femmes, you know. Sally taught me that. Accoutrements are everything, she usta say, and of course I had to ask her what the hell accoutrements were. They're just a fancy word for accessories, which is just a fancy word for earrings and pocketbooks and stuff. Sally was always throwing those fifty-dollar words around when she was mad at me, or mad at being stuck in this peanut-sized town.

Anyway, I don't know anything about accoutrements. I have me an old leather wallet I stick in my back pocket, two pairs of sneakers, and earlobes as unpunctured as the day I was born. But Natalie, boy, I bet she has a jewelry box the size of Montana and a closet full of pretty little heart-breakin' shoes. She was wearing those same silver bracelets that clattered down her arm in a fine racket practically every time she moved. It was like each one of them bracelets wanted to be the first to get down to her wrist. Her lipstick was one shade lighter than yesterday, her smile one shade darker.

"Hi, Honey, sorry I'm late," she said in a voice that let me know she wasn't sorry at all. "Have you been waiting long?"

All my life, I wanted to tell her, just to hear a woman like you call me honey. "Nah, just got here myself," I lied. Both of us knew I had been waiting and would have kept waiting forever and then some if I'd had to.

She slid into the booth, put her purse beside her, and leaned back against the seat looking at me.

"Want some coffee?" I asked.

"I'll have tea," she said and leaned toward me with her elbows on the table as if deciding to have tea was some kinda secret just the two of us was in on. Her blouse moved when she leaned forward, revealing the top of her cleavage, and I almost forgot how to breathe.

"Hey, Freddy, bring this lady a cup of tea," I hollered over my shoulder. Natalie smiled and settled back in the booth and her blouse settled back over her skin and her cleavage disappeared to wherever it is cleavages go when they're not out there calling to you practically by your own name.

Well, we kinda looked at each other again, with me grinning like a fool, 'cause I just couldn't believe I was sitting there in Freddy's with this absolute doll who had come out of nowhere, and her smiling that I-know-what-you're-thinking smile and playing with one of her bracelets.

"So, uh, here we are," I said, always brilliant at making conversation.

"Yes," she said. Not *yeah* or *yep* or *uh-huh,* but *yes.* "Thanks for coming out with me."

"My pleasure," I said, and I hoped she could tell I meant it. "I was sure flattered that you asked me."

Now she smiled a real smile and I could see her beautiful white teeth. She even blushed a little, which only made her more beautiful, 'cause I saw that maybe she wasn't as sure of herself as she thought she was.

"I didn't know if you'd be glad or not. But when that boy behind the counter at the deli called your name, I knew it would be easy to find you. How many Zoeys could there be at the fire department of a town this size?" She waved her hand around like the whole town was sitting in Freddy's, and that set her bracelets rushing back down toward her elbow this time, sounding like a million tiny little bells.

"I'll have to remember to thank Larry next time I see him," I said.

"Yes," she said again. It sounded almost like a gasp, like she had just run into the room and was a little outa breath when she said it. "I wanted to meet you."

"Why?" I asked.

"Because," she said, staring straight into my eyes, "I've always been interested in fires. Ever since I was a little girl."

"Really?" I couldn't believe it.

"Yes. And when I saw you in your uniform," she lowered her eyes and then lifted 'em again, "I knew I could ask you some questions about fires and maybe you'd have the answers." She leaned forward. "Now why, for example, do you sometimes fight fire with fire," she asked, "and why is it sometimes better to soak the flames till everything for miles around is wet through and through? Then I've heard that some fires," she paused, like she was really thinking this out, "some fires burn even hotter when you try to put them out. And some fires can burn for days, weeks, months even, and there's just no stopping them." She started stroking my arm, which felt like it was on fire itself, and her fingertips were soft as feathers. "I thought maybe you could explain," she went on, "why some fires are just warm enough, some burn so hot they destroy you, some go out in a minute, some need to be stoked to keep them going, and some will just burn and burn on their own forever."

"Let's go," I said.

We stood up and I threw two bills down on the table. Freddy was just coming over with Natalie's tea, but we just walked right by him without saying a thing. We didn't say anything to each other either as we walked down the street. I just listened to Natalie's little heels clicking and my heart beating and thought about the fire burning deep inside my belly and wondering how in the world it could ever be put out. I never wanted anybody the way I wanted Natalie right that second and I didn't care if the whole town knew who she was and who I was and what I hoped we was just about to do. It was all I could do not to take her in my arms right there on the street, but hell, this ain't San Francisco. The six blocks between my house and Freddy's seemed like five hundred miles.

Finally we got to my place and my hands were shaking so much I could barely get the key in the lock. There goes my suave bulldyke image, I thought, if I ever had one to begin with. I kept fiddling with that door for what seemed like forever till it finally gave way and we stumbled inside. Or rather, I stumbled. I don't think Natalie's ever stumbled a day in her life. Natalie *entered* my place. She sauntered, sashayed, swished, and swung those beautiful big hips from side to side, checking the place out like it was the Buckingham Palace. We were standing in the living room and she had her back to me, looking at this painting of a sunset that Sally had done. I didn't wanna tell her about Sally. I didn't want her to know I had ever been with another woman or ever would be again. Nothing mattered but this moment. Nothing mattered but her. She filled up my house with all the longing I had ever known and I knew if I didn't have her that second I would burst and maybe even die.

With my heart beating in my throat like a big bullfrog I walked up behind her and cupped my hands under her gorgeous ass. She leaned back slightly, letting her weight settle into my palms, like she was sitting in 'em, and I thought of that song, *He's got the whole world, in his hands.* But just for a minute, 'cause Natalie turned her head and whispered into my neck, "How about showing me where you live, Baby?"

I turned Natalie around and put my mouth on hers for an answer. She was about the most kissable woman I ever met.

And even though I'm no Don Juan or nothing, I've known a few women in my time. None of 'em kissed like Natalie kissed. Natalie sucked, nibbled, bit, chewed, licked, rubbed, stroked, caressed, and damn near danced with those lips. And the things she did with her tongue I don't even have words for. I was dying, I tell you. My knees got all rubbery and I thought they'd give out on me for sure. Finally she, not me, led us to the bedroom, like the tough femme that she was.

But once we got in there, she knew her place. She kicked off her shoes, slid all them damn bracelets off her arm, lay back on my bed, and let me undo her buttons one by one, setting loose her glorious body an inch at a time. Her breasts were round and full as the moon and her nipples were just made for sucking on. She pressed my head into her tits harder and harder till I damn near bit 'em off. I made love to her breasts for hours, weeks, years, it seemed, and that woman just couldn't get enough. Finally she took my hand and put it where it belonged. She was sopping wet, and if I didn't know better, I'd of thought she'd peed on herself.

I took off her pants and her pink lace panties gently, like she was a little baby, instead of the grown-up hot thing that she was. I slid four fingers into her easy, like a diver hitting the water in one clean smooth motion. She took me in all the way, and inside it was soft as ... soft as ... hell, she gave a whole new meaning to the word *soft*. Soft and sweet and wet and wonderful. Oh, I tell you she was all woman from those deep dark chocolate eyes down to the soles of her pretty little feet, and I should know, 'cause I explored every inch of her. I felt like a little kid in a candy store — my eyes just got bigger and bigger and I wanted *everything*. And each kiss I gave her, each touch, each lick, made her catch her breath in the sweetest little gasp, like that was the first time anyone had ever touched her in that spot before. I tell you, some women are just made for loving, and Natalie was one of them, that's for sure.

Well, before I knew it the windows had all filled up with black and a little sliver of a moon was peeking in. I could barely see Natalie's face, though I could feel it an inch from mine. Maybe that's why I let what happened happen. 'Cause before I knew anything, there I was, flat on my back with Natalie up above me, unbuttoning my shirt and sliding my jeans down.

Now, I'm usually clear about who's the butch and who's the femme and I like my women to just lay back and enjoy themselves while I give 'em what they want. That's how I always get my pleasure, from giving pleasure. That's the way it's always been, the way it's always gonna be, and that's the way I like it. But Natalie had me under a spell, I tell ya. My whole body just wanted to leap right into her mouth — breasts, belly, legs, elbows, you name it. So when she finally reached for me down there, I didn't give her my usual "No thanks, Babe." I let her.

Listen, I sure don't want this getting 'round the PTA or even to my friends who are queer like me, 'cause it is a known fact, in certain circles anyway, that Zoey B. Jackson is a proper old-fashioned stone bulldyke that doesn't flip for nobody. I ain't never been a rollover butch, but that night stands apart like it was a whole lifetime by itself, or a dream maybe, or a visit to another planet. No one I knew knew Natalie or ever would. My instincts told me that. And that I was safe with her. And that for some reason beyond what I could understand, I needed her to do to me what no one else had done, though more than a few had tried.

"Silky," she whispered, as her fingers stroked my cunt. "You're as soft as silk, see? This is what you feel like." And she took her panties, which turned out to be real silk, and rubbed 'em all over my body. I went wild, I tell you. Then she kissed my breasts, my belly, my thighs, and finally my pussy, and when her tongue touched me down there I thought they'd have to pick me up off the floor in a million little pieces. I wondered why it had taken me forty-two years to lay myself down for a woman. I sure hoped all the women I ever made love to had felt that good. Just thinking about it got me even more excited and before I knew what was happening, my whole body exploded like the fireworks they set off down by the high school on the Fourth of July and I was gasping and moaning and carrying on like a banshee.

I felt a little shy then, but Natalie just laughed and came up to kiss me. I smelled myself on her face and tasted myself on her lips and I tell you that just got me going all over again. I'm usually a once-a-night girl — I don't need all that much to keep me satisfied, but that night I lost track of how many times I did it to Natalie and she did it to me and we did it to each other. Once Natalie even did it to herself. She slid her fingers into her cunt and took 'em out and rubbed her juices all over herself, slow and easy, never taking her eyes away from mine for a second. Then she reached inside herself again and painted me too. Then she licked me clean, all over, till my legs swallowed up her face again.

What a night. I tell you we didn't even think about getting any sleep till about six a.m., when the windows were a pale pink and the birds were singing their wake-up songs in the trees. I held Natalie tight and she laid her head against my chest and filled up my arms with all the sweetness in the whole world. I fell asleep with one of her legs braided in between mine and her soft breath tickling the base of my neck.

When I woke up hours later with the sun washing my face with heat, she was gone. Gone. I couldn't believe it. Lock, stock, and pocketbook, gone. I got up and paced around the house, fooling myself every two minutes. Oh, she must be in the bathroom, I'd tell myself and go looking. Or maybe she's in the kitchen making coffee. Nope. Maybe she's in the spare room looking at my stuff, spying on me. I wouldn't mind. But it was useless. She was gone. I climbed back into bed, forlorn as a big-pawed puppy whose owner had just hollered at him to go on home.

I stretched flat out on my back with my hands behind my head, thinking. I could still smell her, hell, I could practically still *taste* her in my mouth. I wanted her again so badly I almost touched myself. I don't want this going no further than you, me, and the lamppost, but I even cried a little. Just a tear or two leaking out the corner of my eye. I buried my face in her pillow then, the pillow she'd slept on, that still smelled like her fancy perfume. And when I turned over and reached my hands up under my head again, I felt something cold, round, and hard. One of Natalie's bracelets. She'd either forgotten it or left it under the pillow on purpose, for me.

I put it on, then took it right off. It looked silly, like an ankle bracelet on a dinosaur. I've never worn a bracelet or a ring or a necklace in my whole life. But when I got dressed later, I surprised myself and put it on again, just to keep her near me, you know. Besides, I liked the feel of that bracelet sliding up and down my arm like a kid on a water slide. I pretended like we was going steady and I wished I had given Natalie something. I probably would've if she'd stuck around a little longer. Or maybe what I had given her was enough.

So that's what happened to me, Zoey B. Jackson, on the twelfth of May. It's a true story and here's the bracelet to prove it. Funny, I feel almost naked without it, wear it all the time now, case she comes back. Well, that's not really why. I guess I know Natalie ain't gonna pass through this town again, 'cept in my dreams. Hell, who knows how long I'm gonna stay in this town anyway? Been thinking I might get myself to San Francisco one of these days, see what Sally's up to. Bet I could get myself a job there and wouldn't that be something, riding up and down those San Francisco hills in a big red fire truck? I ain't really a city person, but I don't know, these past few weeks this town's felt too small all of a sudden, like a sweater that got shrunk in the wash. Al says there's something different about me too but he don't know what. Oh, he noticed the bracelet right off — said it looked real fine and was I gonna start putting out fires in high heels and skirts now? I musta blushed real red when he said that. If only he knew what I knew. And don't you dare tell him.

The helper

♦♦♦♦   *Molly Martin*

I didn't know the cause of the fire at the Club for the
Deaf. It could have been arson, I supposed. Or it could
have been that one of the punks who rented the place for
dances set the fire accidentally. The eighties had arrived, punk
culture was in full swing in San Francisco, and the club was
one of a few places that would accommodate the loud music
punks preferred. Some called it deafening, but club members
appreciated punk music, because they could stand in the
audience and feel the music through the floorboards. Some of
the younger members had adopted the punk style of dress and
begun hanging with the punk crowd.

I knew this because my friend Caroline, who taught sign
language, told me. She was the one who turned me on to the
burn job. She had heard that the electrical wiring had been
damaged by the fire and had to be replaced. I needed the
work, so we made arrangements for me to see the place.

I presented my estimate to the president of the club, a
stocky, bespectacled man whose ability to talk had thrust him
into the role of official communicator with the world of the
hearing. His squeaky voice made me wonder briefly what men
would sound like without the ability to hear their own voices.

"Would you like a helper?" he asked. As long as I could see his lips move, I understood quite well. I hesitated. There are some tasks in the electrical trade that can't be done alone. I would need a helper to pull wire. But I didn't want to be slowed down by someone with no knowledge of the trade. Tradespeople know it takes twice as long to train someone as to do the job yourself. And would this helper be deaf? How would we communicate? The only sign language I knew was "I love you" and the sign for "boring," which reminds me of picking your nose.

"I can't afford to pay anyone," I apologized, enunciating carefully.

"It's okay," he smiled. "When will you start?"

"First thing in the morning."

"Your helper will be here at eight to let you in," he squeaked.

The following day I was greeted by a young woman whose hair was half black and half bleached blonde. One side was shaven in a Marine cut; the other was longer, hanging in strands over one eye. She was dressed in jeans, boots, and a work shirt. We shook hands. She had already written on a little notepad, "My name is Bobbie." She led me upstairs and I secretly watched her solid figure. She was short — perhaps no taller than five feet — but powerful, with a wide back and shoulders. She wore a carpenter's belt with leather pouches on both sides. They framed a seductive round ass. I watched the tools swing on her hips.

I've always been a sucker for women in tool belts. Any sort of leather pouch attached to a belt holding any sort of tool. Even the stocker in the produce section of the supermarket or the gardener with one pair of clippers on her hip would catch my eye. A tool belt implies knowledge, skill, physical ability, deft fingers, usefulness, power. It says, "With these tools, I can do anything."

And that's what Bobbie's face said to me when she turned at the top of the stairs. She smiled and her round face exuded confidence. "Try me," it said. At that moment all my second thoughts were put to rest. She couldn't be older than twenty, I thought. But how self-confident, how eager to learn.

I had done some homework for this job, and now I was relieved to have a plan drawn for the work. I showed it to Bobbie and explained by writing on her notepad, "First we'll put boxes here." I showed her a metal splice box. "Then we'll connect them with pipe, then we'll pull wire through it." She seemed to understand, and I wondered if she'd done electrical work before. I had so many questions, but no good way to ask them.

We began by replacing the service panel that held the old fuses. I let Bobbie start on demolition, while I put together the new materials. She started out doing fine, but when I checked back, she seemed frustrated. The screw she was trying to get out kept stripping.

"Here, let me show you," I said, gently putting my hand over hers.

You know that electric thing that happens between two people when they get turned on to each other? It happened to me and Bobbie right then. I could tell she felt it, too, by the look on her face, sort of surprised. I think for just a fraction of a second we thought we'd been shocked. We both pulled away too fast. Then she smiled. She has a mischievous smile that's a little shy at the same time: one middle tooth crooks over the other in a mouth of fine white teeth and her black eyes sparkle. Then she looked down at the hand that had just touched mine. I got back to work on the screw, showing her how to put pressure on it as you turn to loosen it, but my heart was still pounding.

The next day we began the piping. Most of the work was in the attic, which had a crawl space big enough to walk hunched over in. I found it easier to crawl, though, strapping knee pads around my legs. I found another pair for Bobbie. We placed a few pieces of plywood on the ceiling joists to make movement easier and to keep ourselves from misstepping and falling through the plaster ceiling.

The din of the club pulsed from down below, the jukebox and TV blaring simultaneously. Noise was constant here and one thing that could not be done to excess. At least I was somewhat insulated from the sound by the ceiling. Bobbie and I crawled around above it in our own rough-framed world.

I rigged up a droplight near the center of the attic and carried a flashlight to shine on our work in the dark corners. The bare bulb cast eerie shadows on the old timbers and on our faces and bodies as we struggled to communicate with improvised sign language. I was learning to talk with my body. I would touch Bobbie to get her attention, and a charge ran through me each time my hand reached for her shoulder or her booted foot, or whenever she touched me.

I guess there are some similarities to getting shocked. There is that electric pulse that runs right up your arm and through your heart. But let me tell you, I have been shocked many times and this was much more pleasant and much more exciting. Whenever it happened I wanted to pull Bobbie to me and kiss her, but I was conscious of our student-teacher relationship. Besides, she was so young. To act on the attraction just didn't seem ethical. I resolved to keep my inappropriate impulses under control.

The joists and the rafters above us were black from the fire's smoke, so we were soon covered with soot. Bobbie had soot on her face where she'd wiped sweat away and she looked adorable with a red handkerchief tied around her head. I was so distracted by her presence by then that I could hardly concentrate, and kept measuring pipe wrong. She paid such close attention, I often felt myself flush under her intense gaze. But we soon fell into a rhythm. Bobbie was a good helper and a fast learner. She anticipated my next move and had materials and tools ready for me. She was much more agile than I in that crawl space, where she could almost stand at the apex of the roof.

Sometimes, in rare moments, when I'm working with a good partner, when we establish a routine and things just start to fall into place, work can be like good sex. I bend a complicated series of bends and the pipe fits perfectly. She is ready to screw on the connectors and fit the pipe into place, then strap it down while I measure for the next piece. When you click as a team, you feel competent and efficient, and you share a special connection because you make each other feel good. It must be like working together to make a beautiful piece of art. You can stand back and admire the product of your skill and labor.

And that's what we did. When the last pipe fit neatly into the last box in that attic, we sat back on our plywood and surveyed our creation. "This part is done," I said, drawing my sooty finger across my throat in a sign I thought she'd understand. She smiled then and her hand went up to my face for a moment, then traveled purposefully down to my breast. There it stayed, stroking me, as the other hand opened the buttons on my flannel shirt. In my own struggle to avoid seducing her, I'd never imagined that she might seduce me. I would not have made the first move, but I would not stop her either, and my body had already made its decision. I was shaking with desire.

Bobbie was as skilled a lover as she was a helper, anticipating my desires and taking control. She unbuckled both our tool belts and put them aside. Slowly, almost methodically at first, she began to kiss me. The noises Bobbie made sent a current through my entire body. First a sharp little intake of breath, then a guttural cry would escape her, coming from the depths of her. Her hands held my wrists firmly as if to say, "No more talking now." Suddenly I felt like the student. She rose to her knees and opened my shirt, sucking on each nipple in turn. I was glad she had knee pads.

Then she turned me around so I was on my hands and knees and I was thankful for my own knee pads. She unzipped my jeans and pulled them down over my ass. She pinched my hard nipple, and rubbed my ass. "Please, please touch my cunt," I willed silently, but she only teased me, rubbing my ass and thighs. I suppressed a moan, but realized no one could hear me. Cunt juice trickled down my leg. She scooped it up with her finger and rubbed it on my asshole, teasing me, rubbing her fingers around and around, and then she starts fucking me slowly.

I am shocked. I've never had a lover put a finger in my ass, but it feels too good to stop her. What will she do next? Another finger finds my clitoris. I let myself moan. Then she pushes something into my cunt. Something round and hard. Not her fingers. I can't see what she's using, but it feels good, filling me. She is fucking me, a finger making circles on my clit. I spread my legs as wide as I can with jeans down to my knee pads. I can hear both our voices chorus against the noise below. I stick my ass in the air shamelessly and then I'm coming, coming. Yes yes yes yes yes.

I lie on my side and I can see her now pull from my cunt my own battered ten-inch screwdriver, the rubber-coated handle slick with my juice. She lies down next to me and we kiss tenderly. For a moment I just enjoy the electric pulses that radiate through my body. Then I'm overcome with wanting to make love to her.

I roll over and lie on top of her and begin kissing her mouth. I reach under her work shirt and run my hand over her torso. She wears no bra and when I find the soft little mounds of breasts, more breathy cries escape her. I want to feel her cunt, but force myself to go slow. I unbutton her Levis one button at a time, then slip my hand down into the lush wetness, moving my fingers over her clit and inside her. Before I can do more, she arches her back for a silent moment, then comes with a great howl, crumpling onto our plywood bed.

We lie still, my fingers inside her, as her breathing slows. When her eyes open, they are mischievous again, and she makes a sign. Her hands are fists with crooked index fingers touching each other at the middle knuckle. They move rapidly apart and together. "What does that mean?" I shrug my shoulders and lift my hands in a sign of confusion. I'm already scheming how to draw this job out. We still have all the wire to pull and boxes to make up. She takes the paper from her back pocket and jots on it. I find the flashlight and train it on the pad. It says *electric*.

Down-home blues

✦✦✦✦   *SDiane Bogus*

"Don't fail, do it? Home 'round six. That's something to be thankful for; I just don't look forward to cookin' and carryin' on here after doing it for Miz Harris and her brood every day. Up at the crack of dawn, out on that bus line, mo'ning and evening, coming and going. Every day 'cept Sunday. Don't hardly have no time to get none, or do a decent load of clothes. But I gets here, and brings some vittles for the table. And at least I got somebody to come home to. I got my health — a little stouter than I used to be back home, got a few more gray hairs to dye, but I'm alive. And what's good besides is today Friday; the eagle done flew, I can buy a few mo' things for the house, and I jus' took a letter from my sister Nonella out of the mailbox. I don't reckon I got nothin' to complain about. Hmm. Jordan ain't here. Don't know if I should shout for joy or cry.

"Well, Lord, let me put away these few groceries, change outa this work frock, and get these greens and pork chops on. But first, I'm gonna put me on some down-home music and take a few minutes with myself."

The last time I saw my baby I was in the front row of the church.

The last time I saw my baby, I was in the front row of the
  church.
Lord, she lay so still and I loved her so much.
Lord, if I could lay with her, it'd give me so much bliss
Lord, if I could lay with her, it'd give me so much bliss
I sho' wouldn't have to worry 'bout the coldness of her kiss.

"Sing them blues, girl. *'Last time I saw my baby...'*" Within
the few minutes Annie Mae took to undress, and lotion her
body, part of the secret ritual she performed before stretching
out on the quilted bed, she had already traveled the seven
hundred miles or so between Chicago and Alabama into her
past, remembering the dark dive off an unpaved urban road —
Willie's Stop and Pop. It was in that out-of-the-way blues shack
that she discovered a school of love she had only heard tell of.
It came upon her suddenly and ungraciously, like an elementary school romance. One moment, one lifetime before that
moment, she was a young unmarried woman taking her first
steps out of parental servitude, the next, she was in the throes
of a heart-pounding awakening to a life rhythm and the desires
it pulsed, an awakening to another human being. There it was
all at once, and worse than an elementary school infatuation,
because, she thought, "I's a woman who done lived half her
life without feeling what most girls felt in their teens." Here she
was (to her way of thinking) halfway to the grave before her
honeypot and the hair around it ever got wet. The surprise of
it was embarrassing and delicious.

Annie Mae's walking into Willie's Stop and Pop had been
foreplay to her first, and richest, sexual experience. This tale
she retold herself as she rubbed her dry, crinkled palm over
the surface of her smooth, black-skinned mound, bare of hair
now, the telltale sign of age. She spoke aloud: "When I laid
eyes on you, you looked like the answer to a prayer I didn't
even know I was praying. My throat felt like I wanted to holler
your name even if I didn't know it. I felt a big ol' loud shout
pushing up from inside of me just looking in your face, and

scared as I was of seeing and knowing for sure that you was a woman, I knew I was fixin' to be free of a lonesome wanting."

That's what Annie Mae always remembered as the beginning of the end of a self-imposed chastity that had extended back to before she buried her mother. But by then it wasn't her mother she had to care for. That was over, and her sister, who'd left home years before, and who'd returned only for the funeral, was determined to steer Annie Mae toward a life of her own. So in the wee hours of a southern Saturday night filled with blues and booze, smoke and sin, creepers and sneakers, folk "in the life," she fell out of a seamstress's spinsterhood into a woman's bed.

Walking from table to table, welcoming and clowning with the guests, was cream-colored WillieRuth Butler, the club's owner. Full-bodied, full-chested, soft-talking, cherub-faced, and as worldly as a preacher's daughter, she stopped and stared when she saw the plump yet shapely Annie Mae come through the door.

"People say *I* look like Miss Peaches, the blues singer, but, honey, I ain't got nothing on you. You look like that Bessie Smith, and I always wanted me a woman who looked like Bessie Smith."

Annie Mae savored the memory, stroking across her large, protruding clitoris with an easy glide, talking aloud to the six-foot-five woman of her lost past. "You may have looked like Miss Peaches yourself, but you loved me like a natural bulldagger." She remembered how WillieRuth put her lips to her parts. It was like a baby eating its first food: a whole heapa sloppy sucking, mumbly gumming, and smacking. That's how it was that first time in the back room of WillieRuth's club as the sun came up. Annie Mae just couldn't forget. Her mind flitted between the meeting and the lovemaking, choosing the best parts, the energized, sexual parts:

"You just as fulla juice as you wanna be," said WillieRuth from between Annie Mae's meaty, walnut-colored thighs.

And in the next moment, Annie Mae could see her again standing at the front of the club, leaning slightly on a chair as she continued looking at the compressed, dark plumpness of Annie Mae filling out the low-cut evening gown she'd made for a woman who'd never picked it up. As WillieRuth stared, Annie Mae's face and neck grew warm, blushed invisibly, revealing the heat spreading over the surface of her body in response to WillieRuth's height and build, her lovely, ironic woman's voice, and its contrast to her very male appearance as she posed ever so subtly — in a red silk open-necked men's shirt and tailored pants. Annie Mae did not look away; she figured she'd have to brazen this moment out as she did when she had to collect from untimely customers.

"You must be the kind of woman who know something 'bout what you like," she said glibly, not realizing the full implication, and WillieRuth stepped back, smiling, looking Annie Mae over with intensely knowing eyes. Annie Mae stared with the unpracticed hunger of first love and the savvy of a businesswoman. Meanwhile, with a deliberate move of her pants-pocketed hand to her shirt pocket, practiced and smooth, WillieRuth took out a pack of unfiltered cigarettes. Precisely, she shook two out, offered one to Annie Mae, who refused with a nonjudgmental shake of her head. Though they were blocking entrance traffic, the movement of people to and from the dance floor, and even the brusque busyness of the jaded cocktail waitresses, they never stopped looking at each other for a moment. WillieRuth checked her offer, slipped the cigarettes back into her pocket; a flat-faced gold pinky ring with diamond eyes sparkled in the yellow-and-blue light, as did her wristwatch, which caught momentarily on the sleeve of her shirt.

WillieRuth's reconsideration of the cigarette gambit and her decision not to smoke had not been arbitrary. WillieRuth had found something in Annie Mae's slightly protruded, crystal brown eyes that she wanted to respect. Nonella, who witnessed the entire encounter, excused herself with "Looks like y'all already know each other."

That's just how it happened, Annie Mae recalled. They met, spoke a minute or two, and decided to look in each other's eyes the rest of the night, the rest of WillieRuth's life ... Annie Mae could still hear the deep-throated bass and the stinging wail of the lead guitars as the bullish tones and lyrics drummed against the walls of WillieRuth's lair. And the muffled but daring words of the blues tune that the scrawny red-haired singer belted out:

> *Bulldaggering women, sissy men,*
> *Feels so good; Lord, forgive this sin.*
> *You say I can't be saved?*
> *I guess I'll love womens 'til I go to my grave.*

"I oughta be shame of myself laying up here butt naked thinking 'bout WillieRuth, and fingering my gray-ass pussy like some silly sneakin' teenage girl. But it feels so good sliding up and down. Slippery ... sweet ... this spot. This spot. Oooh. WillieRuth usta say, 'Girl, if you could bottle this sweet stuff, we'd be rich down here in Alabama.' And I would feel shame and proud all at the same time. Hotter than chitlings in Louisiana hot sauce by the time she done licked and turned me into a cat purring for milk. I say, 'Go ahead. Go ahead, now, put your man-thang on and jugg on up in me. Go 'head. I want it!'" WillieRuth didn't jugg her that night, but in times to come, she drove Annie Mae with her dildo's fierce and shameless strokes.

"I do want it. I miss it. Lord, it ain't the same with Jordan. Me and Willie had some times together, rubbing our pussies together, bellies slick with her sweat and my sweat. And, Lord, when she humped me, I thought I would die from the good feeling. She knew how to roll 'round and bump up against my pearl tongue. Umph! Umph! Umph. 'Oh, baby, oh, Williedag-ger.' Yes. That's what I'd say. She didn't mind, neither. That's it. That's it. 'Come on, Williedaddy. Come on, jugg me, bulldaggering woman. Give me what I want. Give me what I want. Yes. Yes. Oh, Jesus. Oh, it's there! It's right here, now, big daddy. Oooooh, yes!'"

◆◆◆◆

Next time you see me
Things won't be the same

"Turn this record player down some. If Jordan had come in here, I probably wouldn't have heard him for the music or all that racket I was makin' moanin' and groanin'. Let me straighten up and hang up my clothes. Put on this ol' house-dress."

I'm gonna be in clover
And I won't even know your name.

"There. Wash my hands, season the chops, and have this food on the table, or at least in the pot, when that man walk in here. Unh, unh, unh. I sho' would have had some fast explainin' to do if he had come in here while I was laying up here squeezing my own big old black nipples like somebody suckin' them, wishin' backwards for the lovin' of a dead woman. But you just have to live with your own secrets, and you tell the one you got what you want them to know. Seem like I oughta be shame of actin' like I ain't got nobody when Jordan out there trying to make some way for us to be happy. But I can't seem to get happy here. But it's gon' be all right. It just take time. Now, heah, I ain't fixin' to feel guilty."

You got me running. You got me hiding.
You got me running, you got me hiding.
You got me run, hide, hide,
Any way you wanta see me go...

Annie Mae busied herself with the food preparation, listening to her blues and thinking. "I'm glad he ain't home. Give me a minute to let loose of my stuff 'fo' he come in here with his. Maybe he got some day work somewhere today. Lord knows, since we moved here from Alabama, we ain't done no better. Except get them people's eyes offa us. Promised he'd marry me like a natural man soon as we got settled, soon as we got a little something for ourselves. A year and a half now and ain't nothin' happen, but he done went from place to place and still can't find no work worth nothing.

"I'm too old for this foolishness. Nearly fifty-seven years old and playactin'. Least livin' the life in Alabama, in spite of what folks had to say, was mo' honest. And I didn't care nothin' about who thought I was guilty. I wasn't. As the Lord is my witness. WillieRuth was my life. Now why I'm gon' kill her? But Jordan thought this move would solve all that 'who shot John' gossip. Lord, if I'd knowed I'd hafta work for white folks, I mighta stayed and lived just like I always did. Sewing and quilting. If I'd knowed what I know now. But I didn't. Phone ringing. Now, who that? Let me turn down this music a minute.

"Hey, here?"

"Hey, yourself, Annie Mae. This Beulah."

"I know who you is, chile. What you want? You know it's 'bout time for Jordan to come in here, and I got to get something cooked and ready to put on the table or that nigger gon' act like he crazy."

"Annie Mae, that's just why I'm calling you, chile. You need to break away from that no-'count, mixed-up-ass woman and come down here for a little while. Let *him* fix his own dinner. You work and slave like you the man. Don't never go out; don't never do nothing but sit 'round up there worrying and crying and fighting with that—"

"Beulah, what I told you 'bout Jordan is 'tween you and me, so don't be throwin' it up in my face. Now, he may be mixed up, and he may be funny-acting, but he got my ass out the stir when they tried to make like I was the one who killed WillieRuth. If it wasn't for Jordan, I'd be sitting my ass up in a

Alabama prison right now. Folks down there didn't like nothing 'bout me and the way I lived, and if I was guilty of abominatin' the Lord, I sho' musta been guilty of murderin', too."

"I know. I know. You done tol' me this story a thousand times, Annie Mae, but I'm tellin' you, Jordan didn't do nothing but use the situation to move in on you—"

"Now, look, Beulah, you strainin' things, and if I was of a mind to come down to your place, you changin' that. Besides, I don't want to hear none of your soothsayer bullshit. Whatever Jordan did to get me is half what I let him do. So that's all for that. And if she got to act like a man to have respect for herself, and if that what it take for her to love me, then, I just got to let it be. I know what she got between her legs."

"Lord ha' mercy, Annie Mae, you too old to be fooling yo'self like you doing. You don't love that woman. You just living with her — him — 'cause you feel you owe him something, 'cause you don't think you can get nobody better, and 'cause you can't go back home. He some makeshift-ass comfort to you 'cause he like some piece of home. Now ain't that the truth?"

"I ain't got to listen to this bullshit, Beulah. Later for you." She hung up. "Give a nigger a nickel's worth of education and a dime's worth of whiskey, and she think she can tell God's fortune. Ain't no use tryin' to get her to understand. Now where was I? Oh, yeah, about to rinse and season them pork chops. Here, let me put on another stack of these tunes."

> *Could be a spoon fulla tea*
> *Could be a spoon fulla your precious love*
> *And that's good enough for me.*
> *That spoon, that spoon, that spoon full...*

Almost immediately, the phone rang again. Annie Mae let it ring. "Ain't no use in calling back, Beulah; I'm just gonna let it ring. You ain't talkin' 'bout nothing I want to hear."

Give me a little spoon of your coffee,
Give me a little spoon of your tea;
Give me a little spoon of...

"Damn. You just ain't gonna let it rest, are you?

"What?" she said into the receiver.

"I apologize, girl. You accept?"

"This must be the seventy times seven the Lord was talkin' 'bout."

"Okay, Annie Mae, I'm really gon' leave it alone once and for all. But I'm gon' ask you one favor."

"What?"

"If you should recognize Jordan for the person *he* really is — in your dreams or somewhere, or if it come to you in a flash — will you let me know?"

"Now, what kind of bullshit is you talkin' now? I'm s'pose to forgive you for talking bad about me and my man, *and* promise to tell you that I'll think bad about him later?"

"No, no, that ain't what I mean—"

"What *do* you mean, Beulah, 'cause I ain't got no time to be bullshitting on this phone. It's nearly eight o'clock and I s'pect Jordan will be here any time now."

"Look, Annie Mae, forget it. Just come on downstairs later on. We gon' have a nice get-together starting about ten-thirty. You can bring Jordan, if *he'll* come."

"I'll see about it."

I got a little red rooster too lazy to crow for day.
I got a little red rooster too lazy to crow for day.
He keeps all the hens in the barnyard upset in every way...

"Ten o'clock. Food cold. He missed the news. We always watch the news together. What the hell I got to cry for? This ain't the first time that he been late. He probably working; found somethin' today. He'll call when he gets a chance. He'll probably come up in here in a few minutes like he always do, hungry, disgusted, and ready to find some peace with me in that bed in yonder."

I'm going up, down, down anyway you let it roll
Yeah, yeah, yeah. You got me doing what you want.
Baby, what you want me to do?

"Let me clear off this table. No sense sitting up here like a fool. I'm going to put me on somethin' nice, go on down to Beulah's, and have me a drink with some folks who know how to have a good time. Now what to wear down there?"

◆◆◆◆

"Look who's here, everybody!" Thin, too light to be thought African-American, Beulah swung the door open with the liberated flare of a drunk. "Annie Mae, come on in! Honey chile, you looking good. Didn't know you had no sequined dress. You look damn good in black. Anybody ever tell you that you resemble Bessie Smith? Here, come on in. I got somebody I want you to meet soon as they get back from the corner store." Whispering, she added, "Where's Jordan?"

"I don't know. He ain't called and didn't come home for dinner."

"That sho' ain't like him," Beulah said, nearly drowned out by the fevered and irate beat of a rap song.

"This music is too loud for me, honey. You gon' have to put me on some down-home music and fix me a drink. And who is this you wanting me to meet? What kinda shit is that when you know I got somebody?"

"Just find what you want to hear, Annie Mae, and put it on. I'll fix you a gin. That's your drink, ain't it? Y'all introduce yourselves to my neighbor, Annie Mae." A few people made polite gestures from where they sat or stood; two others hollered, "What's up?" over the music. Others smiled, but nobody came right over. It wasn't rude; it was protocol. Annie Mae was to make herself at home as they had. At home you did what you wanted to do. Annie Mae nodded at the two

couples who were jumping up and down to the incom-
prehensible rap song, and she used the occasion of Beulah's
walking away to glance around the room to locate the old
forty-fives.

All the furniture in the room had been pushed back against
the walls to make dancing and standing space. The lights were
red, except those shining at the rear of the apartment, in the
kitchen and back bedrooms. Otherwise, the red lights gave
everything the illusion of a mellow, sweltering haze. Annie
Mae noticed that Beulah's seance table and fortune-telling
paraphernalia had been removed from the living room to
elsewhere in the flat. She selected a few dogged blues tunes,
and hoped that she wouldn't make people mad by changing
the groove. After all, she didn't know anyone here except
Beulah. And if Beulah hadn't introduced herself shortly after
Jordan and Annie Mae had moved into the three-story gray-
stone, Annie Mae probably wouldn't have come to know her
for another year, and then only in passing.

Here in Chicago she kept to herself. But down home, she
would have done the same thing Beulah did for a new
neighbor — offer a hand, be friendly, loan the phone. That's
why Annie Mae had come to like her.

Beulah was down-home. Born in Chicago but still down-
home. She was real. Beulah didn't go with women, but loved
hanging out with people in the life. She was their Reader and
Advisor. And though she didn't advertise nowhere, she made
pretty good. The folk she knew looked like they had something, too. Dressed in suits and evening dresses, pairs of
coupled men and coupled women stood talking to each other,
while a few men and women laughed and talked together
with a drink and cigarette in hand. Smoke drifted about like
an eerie dream or an invitation to a seance. This was what
Connie would later call a "throwback party," though the
ill-suited sound of the present blared in the background, as
incongruous and odd as Annie Mae herself felt here among
these strangers.

Gotta find me, gotta find me a part-time love.
I said, I gotta find me,
Gotta find me a part-time love.

"Yes!" said a big voice from behind Beulah's door, as a woman in a blousy, floral pant outfit pushed it open with her foot. Her hair was cropped short in an early sixties afro, and offset by large, sparkling gemlike earrings that matched her outfit. Her eyes were round, bright, sharp, and clear even in the red haze. She was busy taking the room in all at once. "Now, y'all got some righteous music on that silly record player. The party got here while I was gone! But that's all right. That's all right! I got soda, mineral water, and fruit juice. Anybody wanta drink with me?"

She hustled in, two full bags bundled against her, one arm crossed over the other. She was a woman with arms big enough to hold whatever she brought to her breast. In the one free hand she clutched a case of soda with poise and strength. She appeared to be used to doing balancing acts. She was tall, heavyset with light brown skin, cute and masculine at the same time. She resembled Etta James, "Miss Peaches."

"Come on back here, Consuela!" Beulah called from the kitchen. "You, too, Annie Mae!"

Please don't cry; don't cry, honey baby.
Let me dry them sad eyes
And be your little cookie one more time...
Yeah, yeah, yeah, I wanna be,
I just gotta be yo' little cookie crumb,
'Til your good cookie come

"Let me give you a hand," Annie Mae said, numb with memory, everything inside of her starting to throb.

"My name's Connie Kinsman, but everybody except Beulah calls me C.K.," this double of WillieRuth said, sharing her load of groceries as they went into the kitchen. "You must be Ann. Beulah's been telling me a lot about you."

When they got to the kitchen, Beulah was just setting the gin martini she'd made for Annie Mae on the dinette table. "Nothing for you, Connie."

"Damn right," she said. "How the hell you think I'm gonna recover if I'm drinking with your skinny ass every time you look around?" She smiled, then laughed as if she enjoyed letting the cat out of the bag of her life. "But I'll take two of these," she added, winking at Annie Mae as if they were old friends and she had every right to be teasing and familiar with her. "I thought you were joking when you said she looked like what I like."

"I don't joke, Connie. I've got my reputation to protect. People count on me for the right information. Do you know the bets folks have won at the track on my advice?"

"I know that I ain't hit the lottery yet on your advice." Connie twisted the caps off first a mineral water bottle, then a fruit juice bottle, opened the cupboard, pulled down a glass, and poured the two liquids in. She yanked a tray of ice from the nearby refrigerator and popped them up without first running water over the stiff cubes. Then, she plopped three of them into the fizzling mix. Her actions were easy, unpracticed, but unmistakably defining. "Here's to the finest woman I've met in three lifetimes — you. Ann." Connie clicked the heel of her glass on the tip of Annie Mae's, which Annie Mae had picked up in a dumbfounded trance.

"Annie," she said, too quietly, but making a new life for herself out of the old name just as this woman had done the instant she walked through the door and called her Ann. "I'd rather be called Annie."

"No problem. I thought you might. Ol' Skinny Minnie here can tell everything but how people feel."

"Okay, Connie, if you gon' keep picking at my work, you gon' have to go to your room," Beulah joked good-heartedly, but it was clear that Annie Mae was confused. She didn't understand the reference and wondered if Connie had moved in. After all, she did act uncommonly familiar with the house.

"Go to my room? Now, that ain't a bad idea," she said, signaling Beulah with a cock of her head to disappear so that she could be alone with Annie Mae. "Which room?"

"Annie Mae," Beulah started to say, "don't pay this fool no mind," but Annie Mae interrupted her.

"Annie," Annie Mae corrected solemnly. "Call me Annie, Beulah."

Beulah saw, incredulously, that Annie Mae wasn't joking. Her face had dropped two years of care. Her light-colored eyes, though always clear as glass, were misty, filled with something pitiful and sweet, something meek but on a restraining leash. Beulah was stunned. She had known Annie Mae would like to meet Connie, and she knew that Connie might look somewhat like Annie Mae's dead lover, but she thought they'd take more time than this — especially since Annie Mae was still so backwards and country, and Connie was so finger-popping quick, and irritatingly up to date — as old as she was. But Beulah could see now that they had hit it off. Connie was eyeing Annie Mae like they'd be in bed in minutes, and Annie Mae was eyeing Connie like she welcomed ghosts into her life on a daily basis. But that was more Beulah's line.

"One thing's for damn sho'," Beulah said, taking an entire bottle of rum, a can of Coke, and both a nearly empty pack of cigarettes and a fresh, unopened pack from the table, "life don't never get boring, do it?"

"Beulah said tonight was my lucky night," said Connie in a low voice, seeking to charm Annie Mae. "Looks like it could be yours, too." She held Annie Mae in place with a longing and intimate look. She was gambling that Annie Mae was as ready for change as change seemed to be for her.

> *We gonna pitch a booty bumper tonight*
> *We gonna bump and grunt to daylight*
> *We gonna do it 'til we get it right*
> *We gonna pitch a booty bumper tonight*

The blare of the upbeat blues jangled the mood between Connie and Annie Mae. Connie asked, "You want to talk?" She was suddenly tentative, unable to measure the effect of her invitation on Annie Mae, who was studying her oddly from her seat at the table. "In Beulah's sitting room?" she added too hurriedly, as she gestured toward the third of three rooms that opened to the kitchen.

Annie Mae rose without hesitation, saying, "That sounds nice."

In the sitting room, they sat down quietly on a long couch that was covered with a fringed, olive-colored throw cover. They were a space apart. Connie did not speak. Something told her to respect Annie Mae's silence. Yet she now knew that Annie Mae wanted to be close. Without a word, she shifted so as to close the gap between them, putting her hand on the back of the couch, poised above Annie Mae's back and shoulders.

Annie Mae did not move. She was lost in a world of memories, trying to find a place to anchor her vacillating thoughts and feelings, which roamed between the past and the present as she tried to see Connie instead of WillieRuth. But every time she almost spoke to Connie, she saw WillieRuth staring back. For a long time she had been preoccupied with that first moment at Willie's Stop and Pop. But, then, with Connie having moved closer, Annie Mae noticed a tiny brown mole on the left side of Connie's nose. That hadn't been there before. That was new. What am I saying? Hell, no, it wasn't. WillieRuth didn't have a mole. Then she noticed other new things — the way Connie dressed in balloon pants and a blousy top; the way she wore makeup, lipstick and a hint of rouge, and post earrings.

"You ever go to any women's festivals?" Connie dared to break Annie Mae's searching silence, thinking that by now Annie Mae wanted her to lead the conversation.

"What's a woman's festival?" Annie Mae welcomed Connie's question. It returned her to herself. Before long, Connie had told her about women-loving women and the camps they go to to sing and dance and be themselves. To be women together. No, Annie Mae decided, Connie was not WillieRuth. She was all newness and difference.

As she talked, Connie let her hand drop forward over Annie Mae's shoulder so that it grazed her right breast slightly, and she rotated her hips just so. It was a suggestion, the spirit of her sexuality moving in her like one who knew the taste of chitlings sprinkled with Louisiana hot sauce.

Connie's touch confirmed for Annie Mae that she was, indeed, different and new, yet her touch was like home. Connie talked and talked, about parades, and organizations, and stores for people in the life, but not hidden away or secret. It was a long night of wonder, and she never once thought of Jordan.

Now, it was near daybreak. The sky was threatening to lighten. Annie Mae had stretched out on the couch with her head on Connie's lap. She had one of her arms around Connie's waist and back; the other rested on her stomach. Annie Mae felt young again.

Annie Mae had told Connie about Jordan, but not about WillieRuth. There would be time. Time that she could use getting to know how best to please this woman. It certainly wouldn't please her to hear about somebody she looked like whom Annie Mae thought she still loved though she was dead. Nevertheless, she couldn't help but remember the first time when she and WillieRuth had decided to go to that back room. They had sat drinking for just a minute or two, then without signal or words, WillieRuth was tongue-kissing her, licking up and down her neck, sucking her ears, biting her all up and down her shoulder and arms, taking off her dress and her own pants all at the same time. It was all heat and breath. And quick. WillieRuth was thirstier than a desert rat as she hoisted Annie Mae's legs up, knelt down between them on the floor, and just sucked Annie Mae's milky pussy. With WillieRuth it had been easy. This slow start with Connie was easy, too.

Wherever Jordan was, and whenever he came home, Annie Mae had news for him.

Suddenly, Annie Mae thought to do something she never had done before: she unbuttoned Connie's blouse, upended her bra, and let her big, brown-nippled breast drop free. She took it in her mouth and began to suck. When Connie's hand drew her sequined dress up, found her panty top, and entered, searching, finding her hot and protruding clitoris, Annie Mae knew a different love.

Also an island

                    Alana Corsini

— for A.J.

Blame it on the Bethesda Fountain. Or maybe it was the models in winter furs posing in mid-July swelter with the solitary, incongruous gondola bobbing on the pond behind them that released the memory of Jessica with such hot force that Miranda barely had time to find a space on the rim of the fountain pool before her legs gave out.

Desire.

Oh, she could call it heat stroke, or light-headedness due to a skipped breakfast; the polite cover-ups. But ever since she had returned from her business trip to Venice last fall, she had found it more difficult to fool herself. No longer could she pretend that she was sealed off from the tidal surge of her own desire, so long denied, which had finally spilled over in a sixteenth-century Venetian villa.

◆◆◆◆

Miranda worked with a group of art historians, conservators, administrators, and wealthy patrons whose mission was to preserve the monuments of the world from the ravages of modern life and other rude manifestations of time — acid rain, auto emissions, vandals. Millions of dollars were raised and dispersed to reconstruct, resurface, and seal heroic stances fashioned from marble, bronze, porous limestone, and cantilevered steel.

Venice was in particular peril. Pollutants raining from the sky competed with the rising Adriatic to see which would first erode the Byzantine treasures of the faded empire.

When Miranda came down the staircase from her third-floor room in the Pensione Accademia that first morning, she found the proprietor and his son removing the chairs and lamps from the lobby.

"Flood warning, Senora," she was informed. "High water. Full moon. Rain." He shook his head, and with a courtly gesture offered her his hand to lead her up the short flight of stairs into the breakfast room.

The only other guests eating at the early hour were the retired English couple Miranda had met in the drawing room the previous evening and a single woman. She nodded to the couple and crossed to a table at the far side of the room. It was unusual to find another woman alone in Venice. This was not Milan, or even Rome, where brisk, well-dressed business-women made regular appearances. In Venice, languid women were invariably paired with husbands, children, or lovers. Unless she was an art historian. The Accademia — the city's treasure trove — was close by off the Grand Canal. Miranda dismissed the possibility as soon as it occurred to her. This woman did not have the nervous air of focused attention she associated with zealots of the art trade. Her deep-set blue eyes were dreamy; blonde, curly hair haloed her fine head, and her slender body carried none of the tension endemic to a system devoted to footnotes and microfiche.

The woman caught Miranda staring at her and smiled. Miranda, blushing, nodded back and watched as the woman slowly licked the blackberry jam off the morsel of croissant she raised to her lips. Miranda shifted in her chair and poured the *café au lait* with an unsteady hand. The tips of her breasts burned against her blouse.

A sudden commotion rescued Miranda from her discomfort. Under protest, the grandmother tripped across the room in the wake of her grandson, who carried a television set against his narrow chest. Miranda's elementary Italian allowed her to decipher enough to understand that the old woman was being evacuated from her television-watching nest in the corner of the lobby to higher ground in the small room off the kitchen. The woman protested the isolation of the new locale and accused her grandson of being ashamed of her; of not wanting guests to see her; of being too modern and having no respect. Miranda smiled, and ventured a friendly glance across to the other woman and found her haunting eyes already fixed on her, apparently not comprehending or not caring about the family drama being played out in front of them. Again, Miranda felt a hot shock wave through her system and turned away, determined to finish her breakfast quickly without further eye contact with the intense stranger.

When she stood to leave, the woman looked up and waved, as if to say, "Later." Her hand was long and finely tapered, the curved nails buffed and thirsty.

A trickle of water seeped across the lobby near the front desk as Miranda let herself out the ornate door into the rain-dashed courtyard along the canal.

"My name is Jessica."

The hand lit on Miranda's shoulder as she stood in the Plaza St. Marco, facing the Basilica, whose main entrance was draped in green mesh to shield the construction work. Miranda had been gazing at the bronze horses on the portico above the hooded entrance. Copies, of course, she reminded herself. The originals — prized loot from an ancient war with heathen Constantinople — were protected from the elements in the museum. But standing here in the plaza among the tourists on a shell pink afternoon, who would know the difference?

Then the hand had touched her shoulder. And as she turned, not as surprised as she might have been, she looked into those eyes of pearly, watered silk and felt a massive displacement in the center of her chest, like an ocean liner changing course in high seas.

"My name is Jessica," she said in English with an accent Miranda could not place. European. Middle Eastern. Something in between.

"Yes," said Miranda, accepting everything.

"Yes?" Jessica smiled, the corner of her mouth twisting up slightly to the side. "And you?"

"Miranda."

"And what do you think of the Basilica in *chador*, this coy green veil?"

"Necessary. Regrettable."

"Your first time?"

"No. I've been here before. Before the veils, when I was, oh ... young." Miranda realized that they were exactly the same height, and found it disquieting. "This is something of a business trip. You?"

"A side trip from business."

"For pleasure, then."

"Yes." Jessica's quick reply fell off into silence. Bold. Shy. Drifting away.

"Have you had lunch?"

"No. I've been walking, everywhere, getting lost. Over bridges, along canals, through tiny squares with hoards of pigeons. I'm ravenous."

"I know a place with a garden and an arbor not far from the Accademia. You'll like it."

"Yes. Let's go by water."

As they crossed to the side of the Campanile they passed a team of workmen laying out a line of stilted platforms from the quay toward the heart of the plaza.

"What's that for?" asked Jessica, slipping her arm through Miranda's.

"The water's rising. The plaza may flood."

"Have you ever seen that?"

"No." Miranda felt the pressure of Jessica's arm along her side. "See the stage over there between the Basilica and the Doge's Palace? There are performances outside at night. If the plaza floods it will look like they're dancing on water. Flood ballet. Fabulous."

"I love your mouth."

Mista mare. Risotto with squid ink sauce. Garlicky scampi. A wash of rasping white wine. What was in the sea yesterday rested before them, becalmed, course after course; transformed.

"I'm sorry there is no sun," Miranda apologized, taking personal responsibility for the darkening sky. "It's so lovely here when the light filters through the arbor and dapples the table." *And your face, and your extraordinary eyes that now glow as if backlit from an interior, luminous source.*

"It does not matter," Jessica replied with a slight shrug. "The weather will force us inside."

"Let's look at pictures, then." *I want you and I'm not ready and I need old beauty to steady me.*

They walked through the restaurant and onto the narrow quay along the canal, unfurling their umbrellas against the sudden rain. Puddles reached into each other around corners. Doused pigeons huddled on ledges against blue-shuttered windows. The thousand stray cats of the city disappeared into secret dryness, while briny water lapped up to the women's calves as they wound through silent streets.

Under an arched bridge two old women dressed in black beckoned to them. From tiny shops carved from the inside of the bridge, they displayed an assortment of tall rubber boots.

"What size?" asked Miranda, turning toward Jessica.

"Thirty-eight."

"Due, por favore."

Miranda unfolded a 50,000-lira note and watched Jessica lean up against the sheltered wall to pull on her boots. As she rolled up her slim skirt and cocked her knee Miranda could see the long tan stretch of her inner thigh. Wetness spread between her own legs, sending a shiver through her body. A man, sloshing behind them, followed Miranda's gaze along Jessica's body. Miranda stepped in front of Jessica to block her from his view, flashing him a searing stare of anger and possession. The man's gray eyes widened with surprise and interest before he turned away. Shaking, Miranda leaned her shoulder into the dank stones. From behind, she felt the hand press firmly on her lower back, below her waist, and then the words "I am yours."

◆◆◆◆

A stream of students and tourists poured out of the Accademia as the women entered the front marbled hall. The water was rising here, too, but caused no great alarm. In an aquatic city, what is of value is protected in high places.

Miranda led Jessica up and to the right through galleried centuries where spirit had yet to manifest in believable human flesh. It was no time for the serenity of Bellini madonnas, ceremonial Carpaccios, or the sentimental froth of Tiepolo cherubs among pastel clouds. Miranda wanted the passion of Tinteretto, his scarlet-cloaked God creating the animals and fish from a stormy sky and turbulent sea; and saints, in the process of crucifixion, twisting from their nailed-down destinies to look up past their sweaty tormentors to the clear light breaking from above.

"I'm ready," said Miranda, turning toward Jessica, who was watching her in profile through heavy-lidded eyes, waiting.

◆◆◆◆

They slid through the side street as Jessica led the way over a bridge, their skirts rolled to midthigh to escape a drenching. From the crest of the bridge they could see the boats tied along the canal swinging around their moorings like the hands of a clock sweeping time in slow circles before them.

On the other side, fathers met children at the school door to carry them home on their backs along walkways that had become the floor of the sea. Flood horns, mournful, broke the city's silence. Oblivious, a greengrocer stood in his small store in hip boots, selecting tangerines for a customer, the water lapping up to his groin.

On the other side of the bridge, the women turned right along the quay and made their way to the spiked gate of the pensione. The courtyard had become a pond with water up to the arms of wrought-iron chairs by the garden. Miranda wanted to take Jessica in her arms and lie back into the water, trading their awkward slogging gait for a slow stroked glide, side by side, past the silent, half-submerged statues to the palazzo doors.

The rectangular lobby, naked of furnishings, had the feel of a deserted public bath. Wordlessly, the women waded to the front desk, where Jessica reached up into a wooden pigeonhole and extracted her heavy bronze key. They wound their way up the staircase, stepping out of their high black boots on the second landing, leaving them to stand sentinel on the worn, dry carpet as they continued their ascent.

◆◆◆◆

The Murano glass chandelier twirled light through its fantastic form like a frolicsome sea anemone, bathing Jessica's desert-tanned body in soft light on the linen sheets. A brief, now-absent bikini had left narrow white bands across her breasts and hips. Honey limbed, with sea-foam hair, she was a marriage of elements against the intricacies of old lace; an undulating shoreline where sand meets waves, the dark sea depths thrust up on land to bleach in summer sun to bone white, mystical essentials.

"You haven't asked where I am from, where I go," said Jessica.

"I know who you are."

Miranda moves over Jessica and slowly lowers her body onto hers — pink- to brown-circled breast, her white thigh slipping between tan, hipbone hollow into echoing hollows. Left arm seeking the arch of Jessica's spine and entering the passage, her open palm cupping her cool, firm buttocks. Right hand tangled in Jessica's hair as their mouths meet. For long moments, they lie motionless, feeling hearts rise to the surface of skin stretched thin over breastbones, beating like captive bird wings about to take flight.

Slowly, tongues probe the caverns of mouths, a motion of hip bringing padded bone down against rising mound. Sandalwood musk; French scent drawn from ambergris; sweat and spit: the lubricants of desire, distilled to a new essence. The fusion of their bodies so complete neither can bear the separation, the falling away necessary to focus on suddenly irrelevant orgasms.

Miranda rotates Jessica in her arms, laying her on her stomach while cherishing the connection along the length of their bodies. Her tongue in Jessica's ear. A sighing. Her hands stroking along the ribbed riverbed of Jessica's spine, up over the swell of her hips and down between the crack into the wet, viscous, waiting vagina. Tongue and fingers, entering Jessica, moving her to moans and soft cries, weeping.

"What do you want?"

"To be part of you."

A sunburst, spreading through distant stars, explodes inside Miranda's soul. Everything she knew until now of love, longing, and union fits on one fine feather of this cosmic fan, their bodies one slim blade of this infinite unfolding.

They move through the night. Now it is Miranda leaning up against the dark, carved headboard as Jessica licks down her sides, sucking and twirling her nipples. Jessica who sits astride her, fingers inside her womb reaching up to the heart. Miranda looking up, dazed, coming, hardly caring, so enraptured is she by the vision of Jessica above her, the tendriled chandelier behind her magnificent head a tiara of light: a Medusa of desire.

Miranda now, cheeks wet with come along the slippery brine of Jessica's thighs. She turns her head, neck arched like a sea horse's with Jessica's fingers entwined in her own riotous mane of hair, steering her steady from their long-gaited gallop through the deep.

◆◆◆◆

A soiled white bag, soggy almost to sinking, drifted past Miranda, shocking her back to the oppressive heat of the Central Park summer, recalling that Venetian morning after the flood had subsided, when what had been carried by water was left stranded on wet stone.

Miranda had awakened in Jessica's deserted room, from which every trace of her had disappeared, except for her scent on the still-damp sheets. With a cry, Miranda had leapt out of bed, sprung to the long French windows, and thrown back the shutters. Stepping onto the narrow balcony, she gazed down into the courtyard, where the water had receded in the night. From the random debris she made out a broken basket, a head of lettuce, and a child's shoe. The sputtering of a sleek black *motoscafo* drew Miranda's attention to the side of the quay in front of the pensione. The boatman was swinging Jessica's twin tan bags into the bowels of the boat as she stood alongside looking out across the Grand Canal.

"Jessica!"

She turned around slowly. Seeing Miranda naked on the balcony, Jessica smiled and waved, in slow motion, with an open palm, as if she were a mermaid already half submerged, returning to her true home below the waves.

"Wait!"

Jessica shook her head gently. Touching first her heart, she brought her fingertips to her mouth and blew a kiss up to Miranda and was gone, the wake of the powerful black boat sending shock waves against the mossy banks.

✦✦✦

Miranda looked back toward the pond. The models had peeled off their furs, revealing emaciated white bodies in swimsuits bathed in sweat. The gondola had disappeared, returning to the boathouse for the next pair of tourists. And while New York was not Venice, it struck Miranda that Manhattan was also an island, and that a deluge was always possible.

Slowly, Miranda peeled off the aqua jacket of her Saks Fifth Avenue suit. Then the polka-dot silk blouse. Standing, she stepped gracefully out of her matching suit skirt and kicked off the black patent leather pumps. She stepped over the rim of the pond and waded to the waterfall cascading over the lip of the freshly restored fountain. Standing amid bobbing toy boats and floating popcorn boxes she let the water sluice over her body. It being New York and not Venice, no one noticed, and the police did not touch her.

Habits

✦✦✦✦

Willyce Kim

L ooking back on it all now, Thalie was the most beautiful
woman I had ever laid. It started as a joke. The entire
evening, I mean. I remember it as a cool Thursday night. There
was a real bite to the air. The bus was late, which was not
unusual. I lit a cigarette and squinted into the distance searching
the horizon for signs of rain. It didn't look like rain, but it felt
like rain. We were in the middle of a drought. Every day
hundreds of people like me climbed out of their beds and
opened their windows and gazed off into the blue, blue sky
feeling like it was going to rain. So far, nothing had happened.
The man standing behind me stamped his feet on the pave-
ment. It was that cold. I was glad I had pulled my long overcoat
out of the hall closet. Halfway down the apartment staircase I
remembered my scarf, and ran back for it. I looked around and
caught a glimpse of myself in a storefront window. I didn't look
so bad for someone who was going to spend her twenty-ninth
birthday with a whore.

Now don't get me wrong, this is not something that I do all
the time. First, it costs money, and I usually don't have that to
burn. More importantly, though, I am not talking cheap whore.
I am not even talking street whore. I'm talking the kind your

father dreamt about as he lay sweating next to your mother on a warm summer night. You know the type. The kind who wears hundred-dollar-an-ounce perfume, and soaks for days in milk baths just to make you feel good. The kind who drapes herself across a chair, legs spread ever so slightly; who doesn't even blow a smoke ring across the room for less than two hundred dollars. The kind of woman you dream about having just once in your lifetime.

None of this was my idea. It came as a complete surprise. Glo, my main slam, bought this night for me through her brother Jerry, the biggest professional loafer in the world. Jerry was thirty-five years old and never worked a day in his life. He often showed up, though, at Glo's place with a wad of money as big as my fist. I always thought he was a syndicate man. He wore pin-striped suits, smoked Shermans, and claimed to have a line tapped into every piece of live action in the city. Drugs? Jerry could be over in twenty minutes with a bagful. Gambling? If it moved he could get you odds. Women? Whatever rang your chimes Jerry could deliver. And that's where Glo got the idea for my birthday present. She and Jerry jokingly called it their major purchase of the year. I found out later that it was a mutual family decision. Over lunch and drinks, Jerry and Glo had kicked around many ideas, none of which seemed to work. That is, until Glo came up with this whore idea, this "freebie," as she drawled, with a hooker who operated out of the Heights.

To tell you the truth, I was far less excited than I thought I would be. But I didn't dare show it. I knew Glo and Jerry had spent a small fortune, and I didn't want to hurt their feelings. What really would have frosted my cake, though, was if they had gotten me a nun. I have always wanted to "make" a nun. Ever since I was fifteen, the thought of my head buried under some novice's skirt in the dark recesses of the cloister, her moans muffled by the rosary beads I had stuffed inside her mouth, could be blamed directly on my Catholic education. Sometimes before I went to sleep, I would masturbate for hours thinking about every nun I knew until I thought my hand was going to drop off. The closest I ever got to a religious experience was when Glo and I had sex in the choir loft of some church we had stumbled upon in downtown Seattle. She went down on me right there, in the middle of the day, her head feverishly rocking to and fro, her eyes closed — lost in a frenzied devotion of their own. When we left, the organ bench was wet, and a group of elderly women had just begun crawling down the center aisle on their knees, from the back of the church to the front altar. Glo lit a candle and winked at me. I remember she looked almost virginal standing there among the statues and marble columns.

I did not know quite what to expect when I knocked on Thalie's door. The address Jerry had given me led to a small hotel located in the middle of one of the most fashionable neighborhoods in the city. As I crossed the street and approached the building, I was hit by a bad case of nerves. I did not want to speak to anyone. Likewise, I hoped no one wanted to speak to me. I ran my fingers through my hair, which suddenly seemed short, and entered a lobby filled with perfectly coiffed men and women. I handed the desk clerk the card Jerry and Glo had given me. He nodded and slid a set of keys across the desk. The room number I wanted was 44. I unknotted my scarf as I stepped into the elevator. I punched the fourth-floor button and watched the overhead panel light up. No one else rode with me. As I walked down the hallway, I wondered whether it would be better to use the keys or knock. What the hell, it was my night, I thought. I would use the keys. When I reached the door, I knocked.

Nothing ever could have prepared me for the next moment. The door swung open, and the most beautiful woman I had ever seen uttered my name and gestured me into the room. I pulled my hands out of my coat pockets and slowly gazed around. A large rectangular beveled mirror hung over an enormous oak dresser. These two items alone filled an entire wall. To the left of that was another doorway, and next to it appeared to be a closet. A small cart holding a collection of liquors and glasses bumped up against an oversized stuffed leather chair. I touched the back of the chair and felt the coolness of the leather. Directly in front of me was the bed. It was flanked by two end tables. An abstract oil painting of various muted colors floated off the wall behind them. It was very pleasing to the eye. I unbuttoned my coat and sat down in the chair. I must have looked like I needed a drink, because I heard a voice behind me say, "Can I pour you a drink?"

I turned my head and hesitatingly replied, "I don't think so."

A hand lightly patted me on the shoulder. "Let me fix you something. It would please me to make you something. Let me please you."

Objects in front of me began to swim. I fumbled for my pack of cigarettes. This woman had an accent. It was very subtle, but it was there. "French?" I asked.

"French-Canadian," she laughed. "What will it be?"

"Is there any Bombay Sapphire?"

"Yes."

"Martini, then. Stirred, not shaken."

"Fine choice," she said. There was a hint of approval in her voice.

I drew hard on my cigarette and watched this woman cross the room. She had the kind of walk that made you ache. Her chestnut hair was shoulder length. It bounced against the back of her dress whenever she moved. Her eyes, light brown and almond-shaped, were offset by high, rouged cheekbones. A thin line of lipstick covered her mouth. Around her neck hung a single strand of pearls. She was perfect. She was coming toward me wearing a red dress and carrying a pale blue drink. I almost went stone blind looking at her.

"It's good?" she asked, crossing her legs and sitting on the bed.

"Very good," I replied, sipping my drink. "Is that a wet bar, back there?"

"No," she said, shaking her head. "There's a small refrigerator built into the hallway paneling. That's where we keep the frosted glasses and the more exotic liquors."

"I see," I nodded.

"You are very, how shall I say this? Handsome? Beautiful?"

I lowered my eyes and smiled into my drink. "What's your name?" I asked. "Before we go any further, it would be good to know your name."

"It's Thalie. Thalie is short for Nathalie."

I picked the olive out of the martini and flicked it into my mouth. "What do you know about me, Thalie? What did they tell you?" I asked, leaning forward in the chair.

"They told me your name, but you already know that. I think it is a very French name," she said, nodding her head slightly.

"Say it."

"Danielle."

"Again."

"Danielle," she slowly replied.

I took a sip of my drink and then another. Thalie uncrossed her legs and stared at me. For a second, I saw a glimmer of coldness in her eyes. She fingered her pearls and pursed her lips. "They also told me you like tongues. And this...," she said, making a fist in the air.

I smiled and placed my drink on the floor beside me. I felt warm and comfortable in the room. "Tell me something," I said, lighting another cigarette. "Is it true that whores don't kiss on the lips?"

Thalie placed her hand behind her on the bed. "Come here," she said.

"No," I said, removing my scarf and coat, "you come here."

Thalie rose and stood in front of me. She kicked her shoes off and pushed me back into the chair. Raising her dress above her knees, she climbed into my lap. A sweet musky odor rose from between her thighs. She took my hand and slowly ran it down the front of her dress. I looked up at her and could feel my pulse quicken. Crouching, Thalie brushed first one breast and then the other against my face. Her hair rained down on me as she moved above my head, and then her mouth was over mine. She drew my tongue into her mouth and held it there while her lips made tiny sucking noises. I placed a hand on her shoulder and pulled away, but she grabbed my wrist and found my mouth again. I was surprised by her strength and let her finish what she had started. Pressing down on me, Thalie sank us deeper and deeper into the chair. Her tongue darted back and forth into my mouth, until we both were breathless. I lay very still. The room was doing a slow spin. Thalie shook her head from side to side and gathered herself above me. She sat upright and smiled. "What else do you want to know about whores?"

I sat there and gazed up at her. I did not speak for a long time. Instead I wondered how much Glo and Jerry had shelled out for the evening. I knew I was a little drunk when I finally said, "I'm hard. Do you understand what I mean? I'm hard."

Thalie put her hand on my thigh.

"Don't move it. Not yet," I said. "Just sit there, and tell me something."

"Anything," she murmured.

"You ever made it with anybody like me, Thalie? You ever made it with a dyke?"

"I have a client. She lives on the East Coast. Sometimes, I don't see her for many months, but she always returns in the fall. It has been like this for many years. We are like old friends," she shrugged.

I looked at Thalie in disbelief. "Shit," I said.

Thalie placed a finger on my lip. "It's true, all of it. Does it disturb you?"

"Listen," I said, "I don't care. Personally, I think sex should be free."

"Tonight, it is," Thalie said, moving her hand lightly on my thigh.

I reached down and picked up my drink. Hooking one arm around her waist, I tossed the rest of the martini down. Thalie took the empty glass from my hand and put it on the liquor cart. I leaned my head back against the chair as she placed first one, and then two of my fingers into her mouth. She sucked them slowly, in and out, and then guided them up between her legs. "Look," she said, lifting her dress and spreading her thighs. "This is for you."

As long as I live I will never forget this sight. Thalie reached down, pulled apart the lips of her vagina, and then held them wide open for me. I took one finger and slipped it into her. She smiled and shivered slightly. "Danielle," she said, slowly removing my finger and holding it glistening up to the light. "Taste me. I want you to taste me."

What happened next is a little unclear. A sudden wave of nausea engulfed my body. Sometimes, Bombay gin does strange things to me. I felt light-headed and flushed. Staggering to my feet I pushed Thalie back against the bed. "You got any rosary beads?" I yelled. "I don't fuck anybody without rosary beads." Thalie tossed her head back and laughed. She laughed until tears rolled down her face. "Jesus," I said, "I'm drunk." Thalie nodded her head, and pulled a small package out of one of the end table drawers. "What's that," I asked, "rubbers?"

"It's from your friends," she replied, handing it to me.

I turned the package over in my fingers, and stared at it. "Go on," she said, "open it."

Shrugging my shoulders, I tore the wrapping paper off. I lifted the lid and broke into a grin. "You got a black dress, Thalie?" I urgently asked. "You got to have a black dress to go with these," I said, tossing the rosary beads into the center of the bed.

Window-shopping

++++ *Michele LaMarca*

I'm a secretary in the sales office of an aircraft manufac-
turing firm. Frankly, being a secretary is not the most
mind-expanding job. Sitting in front of a computer terminal
eight hours a day can get pretty boring, and there's not much
to distinguish one day from another. Most days I have to look
at the calendar when I come in to be sure what day it is.

My office is somewhat unusual: one big room with the front
wall made entirely of glass. There are no dividers between the
desks, just open space, so there's no privacy, and with the glass
wall, anyone passing by can look in and see the entire office.
And with the bathrooms for the whole section, including the
warehouse, right next door, people pass by all day long. The
others complain it's like working in a fishbowl, but I don't
mind. It gives me a chance to window-shop.

It was quitting time on a Friday afternoon, and I had just
finished typing the fifth draft of a sales proposal when I saw
her walk by, headed for the bathroom.

Because of the kind of work they do, the girls in the
warehouse dress casually: jeans, sweatshirts, sneakers. I'd love
to be able to wear clothes like that to work, but I'm not
allowed.

Working in a department that deals directly with the public, I have to dress accordingly. I'd feel more comfortable in a pair of slacks, but to my manager, the only acceptable clothing is a business suit and heels. I know many women enjoy dressing this way, but I hate it. I find the clothes suffocating, and the first thing I do when I get home at night is take them off. For a while I'd been contemplating what it would be like to take them off with her.

She was about five feet six, no older than twenty-two, with jet black hair cut in a short punk style. The first thing I'd noticed about her were her hands. She had such long, thin fingers. I'd dreamed of those fingers moving over my body.

I'm attracted to younger women, especially women in their early twenties. There's such a perfection to their bodies at that age. Firm young breasts, naturally good muscle tone. Their soft, supple skin reacts almost instinctively to touch, and there's a glow about them that comes only from youth. More important, they're so open about their sexuality.

Most of the young women I meet are in college, and many are active in the gay rights movement. It still amazes me that there are gay organizations on college campuses. That kind of thing didn't exist in my day. Today's young gays aren't afraid to say who they really are. They almost make me wish I were twenty again.

I may not be twenty anymore, but I keep myself in good physical shape, and it's my good fortune that the young women I find attractive find me attractive, too. Sometimes when we're making love I realize I'm almost old enough to be their mother, but since my intentions toward them are anything but maternal, I don't dwell on it for very long. I never feel more alive than when I'm with a young lover.

I have to admit I was feeling like a teenager where she was concerned. I hadn't been this infatuated with a woman for a long time. Each time I saw her go by, I stopped what I was doing so I could watch her until she was out of sight. Seeing her pass by my window had become the high point of my day, and although we'd had sex countless times in my imagination, I had yet to even speak to her.

I guess I just didn't want to spoil my fantasy. As long as I didn't know anything about her, I could continue to play those pornographic videos inside my head starring the two of us. I knew once I spoke to her I'd probably find out she was straight. You only have to talk with a woman for five minutes to find that out. Virtually the second sentence out of most straight women's mouths begins "My boyfriend," "My fiancé," or "My husband," which doesn't leave us much to talk about. I knew if I heard those words from her I'd never be able to look at her the same way again.

It's always risky trying to connect with women you meet on the job. If you guess wrong it can be very awkward, embarrassing, even dangerous. With some straight women, coming on to them is akin to sexual assault, so I don't go looking for trouble. I want to keep my job, and within my department homophobia has been raised to an art form.

For instance, when the subject of homosexuality was mentioned once in the office, my department manager, Mrs. Rudy, a newlywed in her early thirties, said the thought of two men together was ridiculous, but two women together, that was disgusting. She said the mere thought of it made her want to throw up.

Not the most enlightened woman, and, unfortunately, she isn't alone. I know if management found out I was gay they'd find some reason to fire me, so I've made it a rule not to get involved with anyone I might meet here. But that was before I saw my dream girl from the warehouse. She had me ready to break my own rule. That afternoon when I saw her going down to the bathroom, I left my desk and followed her.

It's a small bathroom, just two stalls, a sink, and a little sofa just inside the door. She was washing her hands when I came in, and when she looked up, her reflection in the mirror almost took my breath away. It was my first direct look at her, and I was stunned by how beautiful she was.

Violet eyes, flawless skin, and a sensuous mouth just begging to be kissed.

She was slim and boyish, with just the hint of breasts. Her sweatshirt was two sizes too big, but her jeans fit just right. They were so tight I didn't see how she could move, much less work in them, and just watching her ass move as she bent over the sink produced a throbbing in my crotch. It was all I could do to keep my hands off her.

I offered a polite "Hi." She only nodded at me. Great opening line, I told myself. You really dazzled her. Undaunted, I tried again. "You work in the warehouse, don't you?" I asked.

"That's right," she answered in a smoky voice, pulling paper towels down from the dispenser and drying her hands.

"I thought so. I work in the sales office, the one with the big window."

"I know," she said, "I've seen you."

"Have you?" I asked too anxiously. "I've seen you, too, when you walk past my window coming here."

"I know," she answered again. "I've seen you watching me."

Her eyes bore into mine, making me feel as if she could see right through me. I felt naked, and my cheeks flushed with embarrassment. I couldn't find my voice, so I tried to buy some time by going to the sink and washing my hands, keeping them under the water much longer than necessary.

When I had composed myself enough to speak, I stepped in front of her, reaching for the paper towels. With my back to her I said, "Well, it was nice to finally meet you..."

"Casey," she said, her hands grasping my shoulders. "And I think we've wasted enough time, don't you?" She turned me around to face her and pulled me toward her.

I watched her face come closer and closer, mesmerized by its beauty, until it became a blur and our mouths were joined in a deep kiss.

She took the lead immediately, slipping off my suit jacket and throwing it on the sofa. Then her hands went to my blouse and she began to undo the buttons. "Not here," I said, my eyes moving toward the bathroom door.

She nodded, understanding, and led me into one of the stalls, closing the door behind us. After she had slid the bolt, she quickly finished unbuttoning my blouse.

I was wearing a front-closure bra, and she had it unhooked in seconds, freeing my large breasts. She reached for my nipples, squeezing them between her thumb and forefinger. One of the problems with having large breasts is that there isn't a lot of sensitivity in the nipples, but when Casey touched mine, an electric shock went through me. I gasped, but Casey smothered it with another kiss.

She took my breasts in her hands, weighing them, as if trying to decide which one to choose. Then, having made her decision, she touched her tongue to the nipple of the left one, tantalizing it with short, rapid strokes, her tongue darting in and out like a serpent's. Then she took the nipple completely into her mouth and sucked it. When the nipple was taut, she let it go and her tongue sought my right breast.

Her work on my breasts produced the most incredible sensation. I was on fire, and nowhere was the heat greater than between my legs. I reached under her sweatshirt, touching her bare breasts for only a second before she took my hands away. So that was the way she wanted to play. I wasn't going to be allowed to touch her, at least not until she was ready. I relented, satisfied to let her have her way.

Casey began to bite my nipple, and the fire between my legs became an uncontrollable blaze. With no fear of interruption, she lifted my skirt, pushing it up over my hips and leaving it rumpled at my waist. She took down my pantyhose, her motions slow and deliberate, then holding me by the hips, she sank to her knees, her tongue sliding sensually over my belly as it moved down to my bush. When I felt her snake's tongue dart inside me I cried out, and Casey pushed me back against the wall of the stall. The cold tile hitting my bare ass was like the shock of ice on a fevered brow and I had to catch my breath.

For a moment I forgot myself and tried to instruct her in what would give me more pleasure. I put my hands on her head to direct her, but again she pushed them away, not caring what I wanted. I put my hands down at my sides and surrendered myself to her, letting her do with me what she wished. She was cruel, her tongue leading me time and time again to the brink of orgasm, only to withdraw, leaving my body trembling with excitement and need.

How had someone so young learned so much? I wondered, so lost in pleasure that time stood still and I barely remembered where I was until I heard the sound of the bathroom door opening. "Someone came in," I whispered. If Casey heard me she gave no sign, and continued her exquisite torture.

"We've got to stop," I managed through a moan, barely able to force the words out. I heard the door of the other stall open and someone go inside. Casey stopped, then stood up and moved behind me, reaching around me to take hold of my nipples. My breasts were throbbing and I was breathing rapidly, my body vibrating from the need to continue our union. Hurry up, will you? I wanted to scream at the woman in the next stall. Then I felt Casey's fingers slip inside me and begin to rub my swollen clit.

"Not—" I started, but Casey put her hand over my mouth and began to move against me. I could feel the heat of her body right through her jeans. She thrust her hips forward so the rough denim rubbed my bare ass, heightening my sensations as she increased the movement of her fingers inside me. I knew it was dangerous to continue this while the other woman was still in the room, yet I knew I couldn't stop until it was finished.

Casey's hand over my mouth had not taken away my will. It had freed me to finally make my fantasies real. I had never been so aroused, and the danger of our being discovered in the act only made it more exciting.

I became more animated, pressing my body against hers, squeezing my legs together, finding her rhythm until our bodies were moving in unison. I began to moan under her hand, and as my moans grew louder she increased her pressure on my clit. When I came it was with such force that I bit Casey's fingers to keep from screaming. The orgasm was so intense, I think I almost fainted. I know I would have fallen if she hadn't been holding me.

After I had recovered, Casey took her hand away from my mouth. She turned me around in her arms and we kissed for a long time. Knowing she wouldn't stop me, I put my hands under her sweatshirt and massaged her small breasts, delighting in the feel of her hard nipples beneath my palms. I unzipped her jeans and slid them off her slim hips and down her legs. Our bellies touching, I reached down and grasped the cheeks of her ass, holding them in my hands while we moved against each other.

The toilet in the next stall flushed and the stall door opened. We heard water running in the sink, then the outside door opened and closed. We were finally alone again. Things between us were far from over, but we decided to go back to my apartment, where we wouldn't be disturbed.

We began getting dressed. Casey pulled on her jeans, but I required more extensive repairs. There was a run in my pantyhose, and my skirt had been worked around so the zipper was now in front. I turned it to the back, then brought my skirt down, trying without success to smooth out its mass of wrinkles.

When I started to hook my bra, Casey stopped me, saying, "Let me do it." She reached out for me, but her hands never touched my bra. Instead, she took my tender breasts in her hands and gently kissed the nipples. She looked up at me and smiled, her eyes sending me an unmistakable invitation. I smiled back and unzipped her jeans.

It was another hour before we left the bathroom.

When we finally stepped out into the hall, it was dark. We were the only people left in the building. I needed to get my bag, so Casey followed me to my office. Sitting down at my desk, she looked out into the hallway and remarked, "It's like being in a department store display window."

I nodded and asked, "What would you do if we were alone in a department store after hours?"

"I could tell you," Casey said suggestively, "but I'd rather show you."

"Show me then," I dared her, and she began clearing off my desk.

We would have drawn quite a crowd.

The merry widow

✦✦✦✦ *Diane Ferry*

A re you there?
Sweetheart, is that you?

I hear a noise in the living room, a tinkling of glass, no, perhaps it is the wind chimes on the porch. Perhaps you are blowing your sweet air toward them, teasing me with your presence, with your distance, because, of course, you're never really there. But I need to talk with you tonight, so I'll talk, and you can listen, floating about in the living room, rocking in the chair on the porch, or hovering above me here in my bed.

Remember that night, that last night together? It was your birthday and I brought the merry widow home. I had bought it in that store, Victoria's Secret, you know. Me, entering an upscale lingerie store, just for you. I fingered the pink silk teddies and white polyester camisoles until my eye caught the black lace. It was crotchless and had garter belts and I could see your slender torso encased in it, cunt and rear exposed, framed by the belts. You looked so tasty, saliva filled my mouth. I wondered if you would rebel against wearing such a thing, or if you would rise to the part. I was always wondering about you, you know that, from the first time I saw you in a bright orange suit. We were walking in opposite directions and you moved your dark sunglasses down on your nose and looked me up and down. Aside from the way your eyes took in my body, you looked like a straight chic businesswoman on lunch break. So I wondered, intrigued, if you were checking me out. I followed you into the bank, curious if you would do more than look, and you spoke to me. I asked you where you worked and you said you were a social worker, which I later found out wasn't true. You were a bank teller. Why did you tell me you were a social worker, sweetheart? I never asked you that.

But, anyway, in Victoria's Secret, a salesgirl approached me.

"Can I get something for you today?" she asked through her carefully lipsticked mouth.

Mmmm, yes, I thought. I answered just "Yes, I think I'd like one of these, but I'm not sure of her size."

"Oh, yes," she said. "Those are very nice."

She had a similar build to yours, tall, slender, small breasted, with a wide back, so I asked her her size. We discussed it, and I decided on a thirty-four, which turned out to be perfect.

"Can I get you some black silk stockings to go with it?" she asked me.

The stockings sounded like the final touch, so I sent her off. As she returned with them she asked if I wanted them wrapped. I told her yes, and then she asked, was this for a bridal shower? For a friend?

"No," I smiled. "A birthday. My lover's birthday." I continued smiling at her and I noticed her hands shaking a little as she wrapped it up. I was deliciously aware of being a lesbian among straight women surrounded by the garments of desire. A couple of words and a smile could make her hands shake so. I wished you were there just then so I could touch you lightly at the back of your neck. But the thought of you at home, waiting, not knowing what I was bringing, was, oh, so much better.

Are you listening? Do you remember? Remember opening the box? Your face was lit with delight and horror, then hidden as you leaned forward and your hair fell over it.

"Oh, my God," you said from behind your blonde shield. "I can't wear that."

But I knew you would then; I knew this time I'd guessed correctly.

"Put it on," I said.

And you did. I helped you with the buttons in the back. You slid on the stockings, attached them to the garters. You were laughing, but I was acting all serious. I remember I told you, "Now, it's your birthday and you can't touch me — let me do all the work. Those are the rules." You liked that, didn't you? Maybe you just liked change.

You lay down on the bed, feet spread, knees bent. I stood at the end of the bed looking at you, touching you with my eyes, then leaning over and touching your black silk legs lightly, pausing at the top of each stocking to finger the edge. I ran my hand up one of the garter belts and pressed your laced stomach, moved my face near your cunt and blew a hot breath onto it, then slid my hands back down your legs and stood up.

"Don't stop," you whispered.

You arched your back and stretched your cunt toward me. Drops of juice glistened like tiny pearls against your dark hair. My own cunt answered inside my jeans with blood pumping. My mouth was aching for you. I licked my lips in anticipation of yours and your eyes widened. I wanted to be inside you with my fingers and tongue. I wanted you all around me, fiercely, yes, I wanted you fiercely that night, and I could feel you like an undertow reaching out from beneath that lace and pulling me toward you.

"Oh, no, I'm not stopping, honey, I just wanted to step back and have another look at you in your outfit."

I moved my face to your inner thigh and nibbled the tender area there and you quivered the same way you used to just as you were falling asleep. Once you told me you were dreaming you'd tripped over something and were falling when that happened. Maybe that night you were falling over my teeth, my fingers, which I'd slid up into you. Your hips thrust against my hand, my face; I was drinking you, drinking the pearls from your clit, sinking down deep into you. Your voice sounded distant and windblown.

"Marie, Marie." You were calling my name. And I could hardly hear you through the bucking of your hips. I was chasing your rhythm with my flickering tongue; fingers pushing, pressing up into you, open, hot, and wet. Then you wrapped your legs around my neck, pushed your hips way up, and squeezed as you came, cunt pulsing down and around my hand. I kept eating you and thrusting into you, wanting you more: my clit rubbed against the inside of my jeans and as you rose to come again, I came from the sheer force of you surrounding so much of me, and the hard touch of denim.

We lay there for a little while, and then you started laughing.

"Boy, you sure got hot over a little black lace," you said. That's exactly what you said, remember? And then you made me try it on. We tried it with some of your pumps. We strutted. We laughed. We fell asleep. And I woke up wearing the thing.

Okay, as you know, that wasn't really our last night together, but I like to think it was. The rest were distant. You were distant. And then you were gone. Off to another part of the country, a different life. You never called or wrote with your address. Okay, so we were only together a year, but I loved you, or I think I did. Maybe you died. Maybe that's why I never imagine you somewhere else. You're always hanging around the apartment here with me, messing up my papers when I'm out. You're the noise in the next room when I'm alone. You're the taste of sea breeze that floats by the porch in the middle of the summer. You're leaning over me, fingering my crotch before I go to sleep, sending shivers of desire through my veins. You break glasses in my kitchen and breathe on my wind chimes like tonight. I chase you, like I chased you that night, like I always chased you. Sweetheart, I want you still, and it crosses my mind that maybe I never knew you. And that makes me want you more.

Ah, the wind chimes again, so you're still here. Will you hold me? Will you run your petal-soft lips across my nipples? Will you nibble at them gently, then maybe a little bit harder? Will you curl your fingers up into me, stroking, stroking me until I come down all over you like church bells on Sunday morning? Come inside, sweetheart, don't make me wait like this. It's a beautiful night and I'm too young to be sitting here talking to myself.

Underground fame

✦✦✦✦   *Donna Marie Nowak*

I first saw her during the jazz festival in New Orleans. I was draped across the counter of a smoky bar talking to a pleasant black man with a brilliant white smile, mesmerized by the slow, melodic blues trumpet of his speech. It was one of those surrealistic moments in the wee hours of the morning. Clouds of smoke drifted through the shadowy corners of the bar like amber fog under the spotlights. Through an open outside door came a throaty voice and the vibrant wailing of horns, and the black man with the white smile was saying, "Don't matter if you're a journalist, baby. You still gotta feel. You need pain, child. Experience. Pain is the soul of art." Irritated, I scanned the room where young girls with painted faces and scanty dress sat rigidly on chairs behind the tables of garrulous tourists. They brought to mind the twelve-year-old prostitutes I had seen on the streets of New York, peddling their barely developed bodies. There was the tension of a hunted animal about their chalky, drawn faces. Another cranberry juice was brought to the table, and the white smile dangled in front of me like the smile of the Cheshire Cat. "Now, do you wanna dance? It's $3.50 an hour plus tips." I replied by turning an insolent back to my companion and looked up at the stage, where a curtain rustled. A dancer entered.

She waltzed under the spotlights in a wide black hat, tilted rakishly over her radiant cameo face. Her presence filled space like color on a canvas. The long, tight black dress that encased her slim, graceful limbs would have paid homage to any Southern belle except that it was transparent on both sides and she wore nothing underneath. When she came closer to the light, I could see the fragility of her lovely, wide smile and curls dyed an unnatural shade of gold. She turned sharply on spike heels with staccato rhythm, spinning around the pole in the center of the stage to the beat of the soaring music. Her flexibility and catlike grace betrayed the knowledge of a trained dancer; the choreography was executed with ease. Even the hat became a prop. Her cameo face was shadowed, but I could see that it was beautiful.

"Are you going to start tonight?" the black man repeated.

"Wha—?" I stammered. Then I frowned. I was about to tell him that I could make more in fifteen minutes than these girls would in an hour and that $3.50 was barely enough to pay for the damn cranberry juice I had bought earlier, but I changed my mind. I was alive with excitement, and like a shot in a film, only the stage remained in focus for me. "Who's the dancer?" I asked.

"Dorae? Kid was a runaway," he said. "Came from Kansas, someplace like that. She ain't nothin' but trouble."

Now Dorae was bathed in a soft blue light. Below her a dancer with garishly rouged cheeks and eyes older than her years was giggling coquettishly at the drunken jokes of a man old enough to be her father. She may have been sixteen and she may never have been sixteen. One leg, in a ripped net stocking, was draped over his lap. A heat rose inside me. I hated him. Dorae finished her number, tipping the hat over her face as she froze in a jazz pose, and a few of the painted girls in the back began clapping in an effort to arouse the applause of the preoccupied tourists. I applauded vigorously, my back stiff with a New York–bred attitude of superiority. "She's fabulous."

The black man chuckled deep in his throat. "She's mine."

I looked at him coldly and my heart became a hard, amber stone. He was teetering back in his chair with the full, proud look of ownership, his chest puffed up like a pigeon's. Maybe he wouldn't have that look for long.

There was a murky, swampland feeling to Louisiana, I mused, as I walked back toward the inexpensive boarding-house I was inhabiting on Prytania Street. Large, stately houses of different pastel hues sat back from the wide, shaded avenue of Esplanade, banana trees casting shadows across the wide porches, lamplights illuminating the haunting beauty of the street. I could imagine ghosts of the Old South wandering the verandas. Something mysterious and dark seemed to lurk behind the warm, lazy-spirited exterior of New Orleans: the fathomless soul of voodoo and the wails of lost souls.

"Where y'all off to?" Reginald the desk clerk inquired with a broad smile later that night. I had developed a friendly rapport with the staff of the boardinghouse and was flattered at their fascination with my being a writer from New York. During long, lazy conversations in the wee hours of the morning, they had offered cake and hot tea like old friends at a reunion and I had basked in their hospitality and curiosity.

"I'm doing some private research tonight," I smiled, wink-ing. "I love this place. I can see what a great place it will be to write in!" I glanced at my bag and saw that one of the feather boas I had purchased that night on Bourbon Street was dangling from a package like a fuchsia snake. With it came the corner of a g-string. Hastily shoving them back into the package, I started to descend the stairs with a friendly wave.

"Y'all enjoy your evening! Appears like y'all enjoy every evening!"

At the Blue Angel, a girl with a punky shock of black hair and alabaster skin sat before the mock-theatrical lights of a seedy dressing table applying blue eyeliner in the mirror. Her complexion would have been beautiful, if not for the slightly pinched look that betrayed heavy drug use in the past. Yet she had the mix of hard and soft in her looks that I loved so much, and when she caught my eye in the mirror, her dark almond-shaped eyes crinkled good-naturedly into two half-moons. A black leather jacket was draped over the back of her chair, although it was the middle of July, and an abundance of smoky gray shadows outlined her eyes, fanning out to the temples. "You the new girl?" she asked.

"Yeah. I'm just doing this temporarily," I explained.

The girl snorted. "Aren't we all." She held out her hand. "I'm Apryl. But I go by the name Monique for the stage." A few days earlier I had spotted this girl in the wings of the Blue Angel speaking intimately with another girl, who was very Italian and very pretty. The other girl had sleek black hair rising above her head like a wave and sparkling black eyes. She wore vivid makeup and a red leather jacket. Apryl had lit her cigarette, and even by that simple gesture, which held their expressions in the rosy glow of the flame, I could see they were in love.

"I'm Cynthia. I saw you once before. You were with some Italian girl in the back of the club."

"Sheila? Yeah. Sheila was my lover. We split up."

"You'd do well in New York," I smiled. "I was wondering where the women's scene in this town is."

"There's more of a scene for men here," Apryl said simply. She looked at me in the mirror. "You don't look gay. But who can tell?" Then she sighed deeply and pulled on elbow-length gold gloves. "Yeah, I'm so glad Sheila and I split up. We were practically married for two years. I had her ring." She drew black spiderwebs around the temples of her eyes and lined her mouth with black eyeliner. "I just wish the couple next door wouldn't make love so loudly."

"I'm nervous about working here — I don't know what I'm doing. This is the first time I've danced."

"For real? You look like you dance."

"Yeah, well, I do take dance classes in New York, but I don't strip."

"That where you're from?"

"Yes. I live there. I'm here on assignment covering the jazz festival, but I want some extra money."

Apryl turned to look at me, her eyes brightening with interest. "Wow. Now that's really something. I've always wanted to write, but instead I got into show business. I live with my mom. She's in show business, too. I guess you could say I grew up in show business. Oh, God, I'm leaking." I watched with horrified fascination as she pulled a bloody tampon out from between her legs and threw it into a wastepaper can. The uninhibited intimacy reminded me of seeing a woman give birth.

"What does your mother do?" I asked.

"Oh, nothing really anymore. She used to crew on small-budget films. Mostly erotic stuff. I was modeling corsets when I was fourteen. For a while, I didn't see her much. I was always stoned or something. Now she's like my best friend. Wants to come to the gay clubs with me. It's great. She's kind of like a kid herself." She put on huge gold earrings that picked up and flashed out all the refractions of light like a kaleidoscope.

"What does she think of your stripping?" I asked.

"Oh, she helps me make the costumes. I led a fast life. I was married when I was sixteen, fucking sixteen, you know? But now I'm mellowing out. I believe women are the Earth Mothers and I'm into white witchcraft. It's rampant here. I figure it's time to get something solid in my life."

"Of course," I said, inwardly amused. Leaning into the mirror, I tried imitating the black cobwebs she'd drawn around her eyes, laughing self-consciously when she saw this, and explaining, "I like them."

Apryl giggled and winked at me. "I'll help you make them if you like. They're really easy once you get the hang of it." She took a draw from a cigarette and moved to the chair next to me, taking the black eyeliner pencil from my hand. "Been in the scene long?" Without waiting for me to reply, she continued, "I got involved with my best friend when I was fifteen. It blew my mind. One minute I was teasing her hair and the next minute I was in bed with her. She was a fabulous dancer. Wore thigh-high boots, you know? Then she just vanished. I don't know where she is today." She shrugged, blowing a cloud of smoke over her shoulder. "That was the end of that friendship."

"I saw a girl here who is a fabulous dancer," I enthused, trying desperately not to look at the point of the black liner as it moved toward my eye. "Her name is Dorae. Know her?"

"Dorae? Not much. She usually hangs at the drag bar — you know, where the female impersonator shows are. The queens call Dorae the 'dark angel,' some shit like that."

"Why?"

"Damned if I know."

Suddenly her hand slid suggestively to the top of my thigh and I started, causing her to make a long line of black pencil down my cheek. "Oh, leave it. That looks great," she said. And then she got up, saying, "That's my cue to go on."

My first performance was simple. I wore red lingerie under a clingy black dress and red lace elbow-length gloves, and inside I fantasized that I was a famous actress assuming a mask that would disguise my true identity so that I could move freely among the paparazzi without their realizing the difference. That is the beauty of the chameleon, the gift of adapting to any environment. An entire life can be rewritten in a matter of minutes. For a moment, I thought the disguise would not work. My palms were sweating and I felt heady when I walked out onto the stage among the ghosts of previous dancers. But then I began to dance and a feeling of great liberation came over me. The smoke rose like a veil above the colony of lights and I was recorded in the halls of underground fame.

I looked out over the lights, scanning the eyes of my jaded audience, who stared up at me like fish on beds of ice. These are the eyes that Dorae sees, I thought. The men nursed their beers and regarded me with sullen contempt. A man with kind brown eyes nodded and smiled at me, encouragingly, as if I were telling him a long story through my movements. I smiled back as though I understood. It didn't matter. He was one of them.

◆◆◆◆

The drag shows were near my favorite place in New Orleans, Ripley's Believe It or Not Museum. For hours, I wandered among the collection of oddities that Ripley had assembled over the years. There was the man who could be baked alive, people with seven fingers, individuals who had survived being riddled with bullets or swallowed dozens of metal objects. The unusual and superhuman adorned the interior like a sideshow in a circus; indeed, many of Ripley's humans had headlined in circus freak shows. Sideshow freaks in small traveling circuses had always gripped my imagination, although I had rarely been fortunate to witness them. Once, when I was sixteen, a small circus pitched its tent near the beach town where I was staying with a school friend. The squalid intimacy of the little circus seemed almost preferable to the huge, splashy spectacle of a big-time circus, although I loved them both. The House of Curiosity was a separate admission. The curiosities proved to be an ape that leaned sullenly against a wall and seemed too tired and jaded to react to our scrutiny, nothing like the fierce animal on the poster, and a miniature woman in a separate cage with overbright black eyes who looked at us as if looking through us. I never forgot the look in those eyes and the horror I felt about our fascination. Something about them all gripped my soul, something about their isolation and illusionary quality. A part of me identified with that isolation and feared it at the same time.

It was easy to stroll from bar to bar in New Orleans. In the last one I entered, a fat queen in a blue gown and an ill-fitting red wig was dancing on the stage. She batted enormously long false eyelashes at me and I winked in return. She covered her lack of sexual charisma with humor, yet there was a tinge of the pathetic about her. The crowd was a scattering of tourists and dancers. My eye followed a svelte brunette in red satin, the quintessential torch singer with elbow-length red satin gloves and sparkling black pumps. The lashes were incredibly long, the lips thick, red, and sensual. Pleasurably aroused, I watched the undulations of tight satin as she walked, and then I realized this was a man. "Amazing," I said, shifting on my stool.

"That's not amazing, angel. That's a first-degree witch." I turned to look at the tall man next to me who had offered that comment. He was deeply tanned and dazzlingly handsome in a fashionable white suit. The transvestite was now straddling a chair, arching her back and rolling her head with deliberate sensuality, exuding a theatricalism as polished as a cabaret performer's. Before I had a chance to ask if he meant that literally, the man was digging in his briefcase for something. My eyes traveled back to the drag queen again and she caught my gaze with one of her flashing, dark, hothouse flower eyes, a small smile playing campily about her lips for just an instant.

The man read my attraction. "Works in this go-go bar with other transsexuals," he told me confidentially. "Has friends among the Cajun people in the Swamps." He was now holding a small, thin wooden doll, offering it to me. I started as I looked at it. It had tiny pointed breasts, full lips, and beautiful, dark doe eyes. Gold rings adorned its ears, and a white lace dress, its wooden body.

"Dorae," I whispered. I took the doll reverently and began fingering the tiny gold rings with awe. "What is this doll? She's beautiful. I love her. She looks like someone I know. When I was a kid, I used to collect dolls. I even had one of Henry VIII from England but—"

"This isn't a doll, baby. It's a good-luck charm. We call her the Dark Angel."

A million questions began to race through my mind, but the man was rising and making his way out of the bar. I rose to dart after him, but was blocked by a masculine waitress with cheap makeup and an even cheaper wig. "Relax, sugar. There's a five-dollar cover and you haven't even touched your drink. Enjoy the show."

"Who was that man?"

"He runs tours 'round here." The waitress threw her hair over her shoulder, a feminine gesture that could have been natural or could have been practiced. "Don't know him much."

My heart was beating rapidly, but applause and whistles diverted my attention to the stage. The fat queen had begun to unveil, revealing pendulous breasts and smooth skin. "These are the best drag queens I've ever seen," I said.

The waitress now curled her upper lip, offended. "This is no drag show, baby doll." She gestured at her figure, primping like Mae West. "This is twenty-four hours a day."

I was about to ask her about the doll when a sweet, soft voice beside me carried calmly over the air. "How are you doin', baby doll?" The waitress widened her eyes and embraced a startlingly pretty blonde woman who made my heart stop momentarily. It was Dorae.

For months afterward, I relived that first meeting with Dorae. Many of my moments with her seemed registered in my mind like a series of stills from a film: vivid, beautiful, and larger than life. She had flashed me a brilliant smile as she spoke animatedly with the drag queen and intimately I appraised her flawless skin, a complexion that was as beautiful and natural as candlelight without the need of an airbrush. The squalor and clamor of the room and the people posturing within it seemed to no longer exist, and all that remained was this blonde goddess with eyes as dark and deep as moonlit flowers. Lust filled me, and a bond beyond mere lust was formed. I felt suddenly hot and delirious and as if the slightest indiscretion on my part would betray my feelings like a car's headlights flashing against the landscape. "You're a dancer at the Blue Angel, aren't you?" I said softly. "I just started there myself. I've watched you dance. You're incredibly good."

"Well, thank you." Dorae turned to look at me. Then with a friendliness and lack of pretension that I was unaccustomed to in New York, she said, "I was just going to see the female mud wrestlers. Wouldn't y'all like to come?"

Later Dorae said to me, "You seem like a nice girl. I'd like to invite you to my home." Our conversation flowed easily, as though we had been the best of friends for years. I told her about my writing, for which she displayed immense enthusiasm, and I learned that she had indeed been trained as a dancer. "Look, I grew up in foster homes," she said. "I didn't have time to go to auditions. I don't sing, I don't act. I just dance. You can't dance on the streets, not if you want to really survive." We had stopped to watch a jazz band performing on the street and two black children who tap-danced on a board to the delight of the carousing tourists. Although I had always turned a jaded eye toward street talent in Manhattan, I now threw a dollar in the basket for the spirited band. "You think it's fun to grow up on the street?" Dorae continued. "I've seen things no one's ever seen before."

"But you do have a family?"

"Yes, I'm adopted." Then Dorae gave me one of her brilliant smiles, warmth radiating across the cameo face. "You'll meet my father. He'll like you. He's very intellectual and he'd love to meet a writer."

Dorae's house was in the Garden District near the boarding-house I was staying at on Prytania Street. "My father's working on the house right now, so you'll have to excuse it," she said.

"Listen, I live in a two-by-four in Manhattan. I'm used to clutter," I laughed.

A wrought-iron fence surrounded the large square house, which looked pre-Civil War with its wide porch, long shuttered windows, and thick columns, and there was a small garden with a banana tree. The paint on the house was dilapidated, frayed, like the remnants of past finery. When I walked through the front doors, I was startled to see the cathedral ceilings painted with exquisite scenes like the inside dome of a church and the rooms filled with expensive furnishings and artwork.

"Jesus, it's like the Metropolitan Museum of Art," I said. "This is your house?!"

"My father's an artist," Dorae said, simply. "None of these things are *mine.*"

A sweeping staircase faced the foyer and I saw that the rest of the house was also filled with magnificent furnishings, though it was in the middle of a promising renovation to retain perhaps some of the authenticity of the house's past. All my New York snobbism about the backwardness of the South and the superiority of the city dimmed in the light of this magnificence and wealth. It was a wealth I had never touched in my frantic, cosmopolitan existence, where I changed cramped apartments as often as I changed shoes and gained a wealth of colorful experience without ever possessing any real capital.

"My father sometimes runs tours through the house," Dorae explained. "People like to see what the past was like in New Orleans."

Before I could get over my initial shock at finding this exquisite but streetwise stripper living in a landmark, I was further rattled to see a wizened, little old man with a white moustache and a balding head scurry out like a field mouse to greet me with a wide, red-lipped smile.

"This is my father, Dennis," Dorae said. Then this exquisite beauty who had gyrated sultrily in the smoke-filled bar and circled her carmine nipples with a dampened finger suddenly exhibited the breathless enthusiasm of a little girl. "This is Cynthia and she's a writer, a real writer!"

◆◆◆◆

The incongruities in this tiny intellectual churchmouse of a man's paternity of the sultry, Latin Dorae were overwhelming, yet I was fascinated by Dennis's quick conversation. His knowledge of literature and art and politics was stimulating and a welcome find for me, and he possessed none of the encumbrances of a southern drawl, having hailed from the north.

Dorae paced nervously as he absorbed me with his theories on Marxism and religion. "I've been reading *Of Human Bondage,*" I told Dennis, wanting to terminate our conversation for Dorae's sake, yet irrepressibly intrigued. I stood up and moved toward the doorway of the living room. Dorae's apparent jealousy and unease touched and flattered me, although I was also puzzled by it, as if some deeper apprehension surrounded the conversation than I could understand.

"*Of Human Bondage?*" Dorae put in. "Sounds kinky." Her upper lip curled sensually, giving her mouth the soft fullness of a rose.

I laughed. "Actually, it's a classic."

Dennis chuckled and patted Dorae's head fondly, a caress that Dorae rebuffed half teasingly and half resentfully. "Dorae was my daughter's best friend," he explained. "When I saw this charming little creature come through that door at twelve, heartbreakingly beautiful, I knew I wanted to paint her."

"Let's go upstairs before he chews your ear off," Dorae said, making a face at him. She looked at me worriedly as we climbed the stairs and said, "Do you like talking to Dennis? He knows a lot about books."

"He seems like a nice man," I stammered.

"He's an intellectual. I'd like to be an intellectual, too, but I never finished school."

"You're better than an intellectual," I said, trying to control the fervor and surprise in my voice. "Schooling means nothing. My grandparents were self-educated. They never finished grade school. You have nothing to be ashamed of. I think you're very bright and talented. I could never dance like you, not after years of classes. Writing's my gift. Dance is yours."

Dorae turned to me to smile. "You're really a sweet girl. Is that what the women are like in New York? Y'all look fresh and pink like y'all came right from the country. Not pasty and pale like a city girl."

My heart was beating quickly with newfound happiness and there was a delicious throbbing between my thighs as I watched the languid, sensual sway of Dorae's hips as she climbed the stairs. The tawny skin of her graceful limbs was as silky as her complexion and glowed as if infused by an inner heat.

She showed me into a large room at the end of the hall. It held the promise of sweeping beauty with its antique furnishings but, in contrast to the rest of the house, appeared freshly ransacked and burglarized. Clothes and papers littered the floors, and drawers hung open stupidly. Dorae climbed calmly over the clothes. I was aghast to recognize some pieces of paper that winked beneath a chair, soiled by dirty shoeprints. They were blank checks. "It looks like a pigsty, I know," Dorae said. "My life's a little upside down right now. I've been looking for this beautiful leather belt I got in an antique store, and, shit, I can't find it. I think someone stole it."

"I bet if you looked around, you'd find it in here," I said, trying to hide my incredulity as I scanned the disarray. Then my eye was drawn to the posters of beautiful, scantily clad women and the close-ups of the arched torsos of female dancers that adorned the wall.

"Don't be shocked," Dorae said, gesturing toward the wall. "I'm a lesbian."

"So am I." A thin film of sweat coated my palms, and I could barely breathe.

"Really? You don't look gay at all."

That quick dismissal disheartened me. Perhaps she was unaware of the sexual chemistry between us. "Neither do you," I could only say.

"I had a lover living here recently," Dorae continued, as she sorted through a series of albums among the havoc on the floor. Her voice was thick with a childlike resentment. "Only eighteen years old, but beautiful. She cooked and cleaned for me. Took care of me. But she was a lying cunt. The bitch was running around all the time. I think she stole my belt. She stole clothes, stole hearts. I had to throw her out. Now, I don't care anymore." She suddenly looked up at me, black eyes shining eloquently. "Like rock?" she asked sweetly. "I have all kinds of music if you'd like to hear anything. Be my guest."

My gaze was focused listlessly on a slender black vase with a withered rose in it that stood on a shelf above Dorae's massive and clothes-strewn bed. Dorae caught my glance. "My lover gave me that rose and that vase. She had a card to match it with this hot woman in red lace underwear on it. She wore some just like it and gave herself to me for a birthday present. Just like on the card. Boy, was she hot. Just looking at her you wanted to fuck her. She went to live with her aunt now, but she was a runaway. Her mom was a prostitute in Thailand and her dad was an American soldier."

"Poor thing. How sad," I said, at which Dorae snorted. Her lack of compassion startled me, but I listened politely to her heartbreak. My heart churned inside me. I wanted to tell her that when I looked at her, I wanted to fuck her, that no one could be more beautiful than she herself, but it didn't seem to matter.

"She was like a little housewife, though, Cynthia. It's nice when a woman takes care of you like a housewife. But she has to be beautiful, you know?"

"Sure," I said lamely. Then I noticed the picture on the nightstand of two beautiful, black-haired young women with Dorae's moonlit-flower black eyes, high cheekbones, and lush lips. "Who are they?" I asked, pointing.

"My sisters."

"My God. How beautiful. So you have sisters then?" I asked excitedly. "So do I. Two of them. We're very close."

"We all lived in the foster home together, but Dennis didn't adopt them. We aren't as close as sisters should be."

"Why not? Why didn't Dennis adopt them too?"

"I don't know. He didn't like them. Only me. He only wanted me."

Her answer distressed and rattled me. "Maybe there is some way you can reunite ... are your sisters living in Louisiana? Maybe you can—"

"Oh, I see them. We talk all the time. Don't you worry your pretty little head about it." Dorae linked my arm affectionately. "Look at all those worry lines. None of that now." She pulled me toward the staircase. "Is that what they do in Manhattan? Fret and worry..." I noticed the dimple near her chin for the first time. "Look, why don't you stay for dinner? Dennis makes great blackened crawfish, better than you could get in a restaurant. I don't have many friends. All these people who hang around me in the bars — they're not friends. They're barflies and when the night's over, so is the friendship."

I knew I had to work on the article I was writing, but that didn't seem to matter now. I remembered vaguely that I needed to write tonight, because I had a deadline to meet, but my heart was quickening again as if all time were suspended in this moment. I was touched by Dorae's waiflike innocence, a dichotomy against her elegance and street smarts, yet my compassion and instant sense of loyalty toward her was laced with a burning physical desire. When she threw back her head and the tawny curve of her throat glistened like the soft curve of her upper lip, I envisioned my mouth moving across that satin.

"I'd love to stay," I heard myself say.

◆◆◆◆

The evening grew longer and longer as Dennis talked. The New Yorker–like quickness of his manner comforted me, and Dorae relaxed like a goddess in one of the high-backed chairs around the flickering candlelight from the table. "I like things of great beauty," Dennis explained. "My little Dorae inherited my fine taste." He picked up tiny crystal glasses from the table that were tinted a deep shade of lavender. "Dorae brought these as a Christmas present when she was just twelve years old."

Later, as we walked toward the staircase, Dorae said suddenly, "Dennis usually eats too much meat. I try to be a vegetarian. One time I made a lot of eggs for him, because I figured he'd have a heart attack with all the cholesterol. I wanted to poison him."

"Why would you want to poison him?!" I was visibly rattled. What other surprises were in store in this Alice-in-Wonderland house where things weren't what they seemed to be?

Dorae smiled soothingly. "Don't worry, honey. He's fit as a fiddle even with all the fat he eats. And you see how smart he is? He took me to Europe when I was just fifteen, just as if I was his real daughter. Without him, I probably would have been dead. No one else cared."

"Then why did you want to poison him?" I persisted.

"Because he can be a pain in the ass. You don't see that side." Dorae turned to look at me and grabbed my hand with an affectionate squeeze. "You're staying over. It's not safe to walk home now. Dennis likes you. It's fine."

"Where will I sleep?"

"In my room, of course. There's a lot of space. You can't tell with the clothes and all, but you'll have your own towel."

I was amused at her ironic but sweet reasoning. A feather-weight happiness was beginning to radiate through me like the drunken high of alcohol. The vague sense that there were things to be done in the morning glimmered momentarily once again in my consciousness and then vanished as quickly as it emerged.

The bathroom was thick with steam and heat, but Dorae's soft musical voice was calling me. "Honey, I want some Epsom salts. Can you bring me some Epsom salts? They're right by the sink and I'm too lazy to move."

I slid open the bathroom door, heart pounding, and spotted the large box of Epsom salts by the vanity. The steambath was turned on and a huge cloud of steam was spiraling through the bathroom. Dorae sat in a large, old-fashioned bathtub like an Egyptian pharaoh, exquisitely erotic, effortlessly beautiful, beads of sweat glistening on her languid face and her yellow curls plastered damply to her forehead. Her black sloe eyes twinkled impishly when I looked at her, and her tawny breasts, with their large carmine nipples, were pointed provocatively at me, lusciously full and erect against her broad and graceful shoulders. "Come on in," she said softly. "The water's fine."

"Epsom salts, tea, or me?" I quipped.

◆◆◆◆

I sat between Dorae's thighs in the steambath, our bodies plastered together, my senses intoxicated by the sweat of her hot, smooth body pressed against mine, the sultry steam, and the whole feminine, musky scent of her. We had left the bath, where we had played footsies in the water and compared body parts and kissed and sucked each other's nipples tantalizingly slowly in extended foreplay. Now, her fingers moved slowly and luxuriously across my vulva, teasing the clitoris, while she cupped my breast with her other hand and fondled the nipple. My body was achingly aroused, filled with exquisite sensations. I arched my back and our lips found each other and I was passionately kissing that soft, full mouth, our tongues meshing together, probing as insistently as her fingers probed my vagina. "I like it this way," Dorae whispered against my ear then. "I like to have control of the woman. I like to be the man."

I giggled at the absurdity of the butch/femme game. "You don't look anything like a man." I groaned as one finger rubbed more insistently against my clitoris. "Oh, shit. I feel like I'm going to come already," I whimpered.

"Not so quickly, darling. Not so quickly," Dorae laughed, biting my earlobe. "Let's go to my room."

Then we moved to the bedroom, our damp bodies clad in open cotton robes, caressing and kissing and clinging to each other and giggling wildly. Dorae tried to carry me and I wound my legs around her. She threw me, laughing, onto the bed and I felt conscious of the misty sultriness of a jungle there in the dark with the cool white cotton of the sheets against my fingertips and the anticipation tingling in my body, aching for release. I wondered vaguely where Dennis was during this lesbian wet dream, but I was drunk with happiness, alive inside my dream. Dorae's gold curls glistened in the dark as she sat at my feet on the bed, an erotic angel. "Lie still. Don't move," she whispered. "I'll come to you."

Then she was moving under the sheet that encased my body and I felt her hands slide up around my hips like satin gloves and shivery, soft lips moving against my thighs and across my stomach. "This is my favorite part of a woman's body. Her womb," she whispered.

"Don't get me pregnant," I said. "Although I'd love to have your children."

Her mouth became hot on my body, her hands insistent. My own hands glided over the satiny smoothness of her body and I wondered how anything in the world could be more beautiful and pleasurable than this woman. My heart and senses filled, spilling over with a happiness that ached as insistently as my clitoris with ecstasy. "You're so beautiful," I whispered into her ear, whimpering with happiness, as her black eyes glistened like jewels under the lowered lashes, her breath hot against my mouth. "You're so fucking beautiful." Then her hot mouth found my clitoris again and her fingers were sliding into my vagina and I cried out as my clit seemed to explode and my body shuddered with the heat of orgasm.

From that time on, Dorae and I spent every available moment together. I worked halfheartedly on my article and supplemented my income working as an office temp and dancing occasionally so that I could stay in New Orleans a bit longer, but nothing seemed to matter as much as my fevered passion for Dorae. I was in love for the first time and I knew that all my lovers, past and future, would pale in comparison with the all-consuming love I had for Dorae. She was sometimes very critical and volatile with me, blaming me for her shortcomings, which I attributed to her troubled childhood, but I could always soothe her outbursts and I was determined to erase the ghosts of her pain through my love. Never before had I been so alive in the present, so happily content in every moment I shared with Dorae. I wanted to tell the world. She called me at odd hours and I dressed in the wee hours of the morning to meet her, even in the rain, drunk on my love, eager to woo her with my heartfelt extravagance.

We went on a swamp tour and the water moved like sheets of undulating glass beneath us, reflecting the dripping boughs of weeping willows as white and blue herons soared above us and crocodiles slowly surfaced in the camouflage of the green water, grinning their ancient, crooked grins. Dorae and I sat closely together, deliriously happy, and as we listened politely to the tour guide, we fondled each other's breasts through an opening in our tunics, undetected by the other tourists, until we were limp with arousal. We ate in expensive Creole restaurants with white linen tablecloths and Dorae kept one foot between my thighs, rubbing my clit with her silk-clad toe, our clandestine encounter invisible to other diners; or we wore no underwear under our summer-light dresses and made love in the stalls of bathrooms or in the stairways of old buildings in the French Quarter, our excitement intensified by the fear of detection.

One night I woke from a dream of the jungle to find myself lying naked on her unmade bed, one hand pressing the heat of her tawny body. An overhead fan was purring above me and long yellow squares of light stretched across the bedroom floor. In the light I saw the glitter of the clutter that Dorae had once asked me to clean for her as her teenaged lover had done. I had been hurt and irritated when she blamed me for her own slovenliness, but attempted to surprise her by cleaning the room. I did it on a Saturday when I should have been writing. The result pleased and excited me, but within a few days the room was again in its familiar disarray.

Dorae smiled at me through the dark. "Go back to sleep, baby," she whispered. She was lying beside me in long johns like a little girl, her face simple and innocent without a trace of makeup. We held each other. "Your mother must have been very beautiful," I said finally.

Dorae's voice was quiet and reflective. "Yes, I'm sure she was. I remember her screwing someone when I was about three years old. Lots of men. She's in an asylum now."

"Have you seen her?"

"Only once. I never want to see her again. She looked like one of those bag people. Sometimes I think I'll end up like her, crazy. Something bad's going to happen to me one day. I know it." A tear slid from the corner of one solemn black eye and slid down her cheek.

"No, nothing will ever happen to you," I told her fervently, hugging her tightly. I was distressed by her unhappiness. "I'll make sure of it."

"There's nothing you can do. Do you know how I've had to survive most of my life, Cynthia? Through my looks. Through strangers. Sometimes I depended on men I met in the bars to support me and—"

"It's over now. You don't have to depend on those creeps in the bars. You have a lot of talent. You don't have to dance in a bar. I want to help you get out of that scene. It's destructive for you."

"No, the scene isn't the problem. It's like being famous. No, the problems are much deeper than that, Cyndy. You don't understand. There's nothing you can do."

"Yes, there is. Help me understand then. I love you."

During the time I spent sleeping at Dorae's house, there was a disturbing tendency for the phone to ring at odd hours.

Dorae would take the calls in another room, where she spoke in whispers. I had begun to realize that while possessing the breathless enthusiasm and quick affection of a child, Dorae also possessed the emotional maturity of a child in some respects, as she left Dennis to entertain me while she disappeared for hours on end. Then one day she said suddenly, "I know a way we could make extra money." She was twisting her hair nervously around her finger, black eyes wide and guilty.

"How?" I asked.

"I have this friend, baby, who would like to see us make love. We don't have to do anything with him. But he's really rich and really stupid and he'll pay us five hundred dollars apiece."

"What?! I'm not going to fuck in front of some creepy man. Who is this guy?!"

"He's an old friend from the bars. He used to have a thing for me. But I never did anything with him. I'd just let him take me out and I'd promise him things."

"Dorae." I grabbed her hand. "You don't need these people. We don't need them. A guy like that could do anything, it's dangerous. Don't you see?" A vein was pulsing in my forehead. "Five hundred dollars isn't worth it! We could get hurt. I don't want to see you get hurt. Promise me—"

"You're making me go straight," she laughed. Then she threw her arms around me. "My sweet baby. I won't call him. You're right. You're really right. Besides, he probably would stiff us for the money anyway."

✦✦✦✦

I was running out of money. The anxiety had begun to gnaw at me like a mouse, but Dennis often prepared great Cajun dinners for us and I was spending more and more of my time there. As long as I was with Dorae, that time seemed justified.

Recently Dennis had entertained some artist friends of his and I had been delighted by the high wit and sparkling conversation. Somewhere in the middle of the evening, Dorae, exquisite in white silk, disappeared, to my disconcertion. Later, I discovered her up in her room, huddled in a ball on her white bed in her finery. The image of this lost child huddled in a fetal position remained vividly in my mind for years to come. "What's the matter?" I asked, worriedly. "What's wrong?"

Tears were streaming down her face and her voice was muffled. "I feel dumb," she said, in her childlike manner. "I have nothing to say to them. They're all intellectuals."

I was holding her tightly, but she hid her face in embarrassment when I tried to kiss away her tears. "No, baby, you're not dumb. Don't ever underestimate yourself. You're as smart and gifted as any of them. Fancy words don't mean a thing."

"I want to know fancy words. I've always been so poor at English."

"I'll help you love books, honey. I'll show you the way."

Later I bought Dorae a colorfully illustrated edition of *The Wizard of Oz*, remembering that my love of literature had begun with pictures, and we worked industriously and secretly at reading a chapter every night, until I discovered that Dorae did everything during the reading hour to sabotage it, finally claiming she wanted to read it herself. She struggled nightly with the chapters at first, one finger moving under the words as her mouth moved with them, until she finally began reading *Penthouse* and *Oui* secretly behind the book's covers.

Now Dorae again seemed distracted at the idea of reading, although I had given her a sexier book to try to capture her attention. She handed me a tight leopard jumpsuit that crossed the body, strapless on one side and full-sleeved on the other, with a zipper on the strapless side. "Put this on," she smiled. "I like to see my women dance for me."

"Why don't you wear something like this? You would look so beautiful in it," I said.

"No way. I wear that stuff all night on the job. I don't want to wear it when I'm not working, too! But I like to see women dressed that way. Put it on and dance for me. Put on the heels and make your eyes very catlike. You'll look good that way. You have nice, big eyes."

I felt the excitement of a little girl inside, a secret satisfaction and pleasure as the soft fabric slid over my body like a glove. "I would never do this for a man. It's so strange," I said. "I'm very nervous."

"Want vodka? Here. Drink some vodka. You'll loosen up," Dorae said. She sat back on her elbows and surveyed me under heavy lids, one lock of hair falling over a steamy black eye.

I drank the vodka, which burned my throat, and then began to dance, giggling. "I'm not really used to this," I said. "You're the one with the experience, sweetie."

"You're doing fine. I like this. Would you get me a drink of water downstairs? Please. You know I'll pay you well when you return." It both amused and annoyed me that Dorae liked to be waited on like a queen. I would never wait on a man, I often considered ironically.

"Okay," I said. I felt embarrassed to appear in front of Dennis, who was sitting at the kitchen table reading *The Persecution of the Jews*. He looked up startled, as if seeing me for the first time, and said, "Don't you look delectable."

I laughed nervously and said, "It's one of Dorae's uniforms." Then I began rummaging through the fridge for the bottled water, which I poured into a glass carefully. I suddenly felt Dennis's hand moving across the open back of my costume and then over my ass, and heard him whisper, "I'd love to eat you. I bet you'd be as sweet as candy." I was startled to see this side of him, although Dorae had told me in a bitter voice that he had come on to her teen lover. It seemed so discordant with his sweet, grandfatherly image and so unlike anyone in my own family. Automatically, I turned and slapped his face.

Distressed, I decided not to mention the incident to Dorae, since it would only upset her and create a huge scene. Dorae smiled at me like a contented lioness when I returned, whispering, "Thank you, darling." She pulled me into her arms, squeezing me tightly against her body and touching shivery soft lips to my ear. "I love the way you feel, baby. You have baby-soft skin." She pushed me down backward on the bed and slowly kissed my neck and shoulders with her soft, sensual mouth as one hand began to slowly unzip the side of my jumpsuit. "I want my nourishment morning, noon, and night."

She took a nipple in her mouth and sucked and licked softly at first and then with increasing ardor, murmuring and moaning. Peaks of pleasure and heat ran through me like white electricity as I arched my back and thrust my breasts against her face. "I love you so much," I whimpered breathlessly. "I love you so much." My fingers massaged her scalp, lightly pulling the silky gold curls, then explored the satin curve of her throat. Her skin was as smooth and hot as the softest sand, glistening beneath the sun with tawny brilliance. Hungrily my fingers sought her breasts beneath her shirt, and she groaned as I rolled her carmine nipples between thumb and forefinger, squeezing gently. I loved to feel the fullness of her warm breasts in my palms and the palpitations of her heart and breath. She was rubbing the head of my clitoris in circular movements with the ball of her finger and I felt the hot agonizing waves of an orgasm blossoming through me. Then she began to finger-fuck me with a savage passion, panting as she clung to me, and roughly twisting my body into different positions. The bittersweet sensations, like a white lightning, shot through my body with the incongruities of a mirage, alternating between pain and pleasure and ultimately indistinguishable as either, as the bed rocked beneath us like a swing.

◆◆◆

"There's blood on your chair," said Apryl. "Do you have your period?"

Nervously, I rubbed the dark stain on the torn seat of my stool at the Blue Angel and rubbed my fingertips together. "No. I don't have my period," I said with concern. "I don't know why I keep bleeding."

"You look sick. I think you should see a doctor," Apryl said. She put her lipstick down on the table with a loud clatter, shaking her head. "Could be a urinary tract thing. I had that problem before, but my lover takes good care of me now." Apryl proudly displayed a photo of an androgynous platinum blonde whose hair rose above her head like a sea wave and who sported an earring in her nose. "She's a fucking knock-out," Apryl enthused. I looked at Apryl's delicate wrists as she held out the photo, delicate wrists like mine. It was that vulnerability in women that at one time I'd wanted to protect and that still aroused me physically and emotionally. Apryl blew a cloud of smoke over her shoulder with a quick jerk of her head, the sort of gesture you see on street punks. She grinned, her eyes crinkling with sexy warmth. I could see her standing on a street corner, wearing loads of eyeshadow prematurely. "Her name's Jeep. She's a high priestess."

"What do you mean, a high priestess?" I asked. My head was throbbing and I felt the sting of fever blisters that were starting to erupt around my mouth. My nerves were jumping. They wouldn't stop.

"You shitting me? It's the highest point you can reach as a witch! Jeep's really up there. I respect her." Apryl held her mouth in an "O" and lined it with orange. Her nails were studded with glittering orange stars. "You know, you seem really strung out lately. Maybe she can help you."

"I didn't get much sleep," I mumbled. "Gee, thanks. I'll — uh — keep her in mind." I couldn't bear to tell her the real reason I was starting to deteriorate: the fact was I was worried about Dorae. And I didn't know how much longer I could last under the strain of our relationship.

One night she had called me in the wee hours of the morning, her voice strained and urgent, and I had dressed hurriedly to meet her. There she was at one of the seedier corners in the Garden District, a suitcase in her hand, her beautiful face pale and eloquent without makeup. "I'm running away," she said. "I'm going to run away from everybody!"

It was a scene I had experienced over and over again without getting any closer to the cause of her anguish beyond some vague notion that it was connected with the ghosts of her past. During those times she hated everyone; hardest to bear, sometimes she would say she even hated me.

"No, baby, no, we'll talk. Just tell me what's bothering you and I can help," I had pleaded.

"I need money. I need a place to stay. Tell me what you can fucking do."

"Well, I'm staying at the boardinghouse. I — I don't think they'd let me stay if I brought someone in, but you can stay there a few nights if we're quiet about it. You know you can stay with me!"

"And what about money?! What about that?! You were supposed to help me learn English, but look at the way you fucked that one up! You didn't do shit! Who needs a lover like that?!"

I was stunned by her accusations, but frantic. I had worked harder to lend Dorae money when she had been too distressed to work for one reason or another, and now my own money situation was desperate. "I tried to help you, Dorae, but I can't force you to read the books — this isn't fair!" My hands were shaking and Dorae grabbed them.

"I don't know what I'm saying." Her voice was quiet, but exhausted. She looked so lost and confused then that I threw my arms around her. "You can't help me, Cynthia," she whispered brokenly in my ear. "You can't help me."

I held onto her tightly. "No, I love you. I can help you. Don't leave me ever, please. Why don't you talk to me?! Please talk to me."

"Look. I'll stay at your place for a few days. We'll be quiet. Everything will be fine." Dorae was smiling then, stroking the side of my face.

So I had moved her bags quietly into the boardinghouse on Prytania Street, and although the nerves were beginning to jump in my head — the same nerves that jumped when Dorae screamed at me suddenly for things that were beyond my control, or took phone calls in whispers and left me alone for hours, or blamed me for the state of her room or her ignorance of literature — a happiness began to radiate through me at the fact that we would be together, and we would resolve all our problems. I felt bruised and exhausted, but a flower was blossoming inside me, a promise of salvation.

And that night we had taken a shower together and soaped each other's backs and Dorae had looked at me with an innocence that broke my heart. Her hands, her silken hands with the broken nails, had held mine with a trust that touched me, and we'd hugged and planted soft bites across each other's bodies in the water, bringing each other to ecstasy over and over. "I thought I had somewhere to go, but now my home with Dennis doesn't feel like home," she'd said. "You have your family, you came from that house. I had nothing, Cynthia. At times I almost wanted to die. But now I have you. Without you, I think I'd go crazy."

"You'll always have me," I'd said, and held her tightly, wanting to never let go.

Now Apryl looked at me. "You look really fucking sick. Are you having a hard time with that Dark Angel broad?"

"She's wonderful," I said. "No. Everything's going to be okay. I'm going to help her. She's had a lot of sadness in her life—"

"You look like *you* fucking need help! Maybe you're catching her sadness! Hey. A lot of people have been in love with that girl. Don't let her break your heart —"

"She's not going to break my heart!" I said defensively. "You don't know her! We're going to get married! She's so sweet—"

"Hey! Don't flip out! I got really sick over someone once. We'd get stoned together. Now I don't touch that shit. I'm clean. I never shot up or anything, though. Hell, no."

Dorae had begun leaving trails of garbage around my room at the boardinghouse, which made me snap with irritation. She was depending on me to get the bulk of our food and then ordering the most expensive things on the menu without having the money to pay for them, or eating the bulk of what I bought for both of us. When I would blow up, her nervous apologies would soften me and make me feel guilty. She was a child, a beautiful child, well meaning but selfish, and I couldn't blame her for her shortcomings knowing the long road she was traveling to escape her childhood nightmares. Yet bearing the weight of responsibility for her was breaking me down, even as I buried my anger under her charm.

"There was a man who had a doll that looked just like you, sweetie," I had told her. "She was beautiful just like you."

"Yeah. I know the guy," Dorae had said, laughing nervously. "He runs tours. He's really into the jungle, life in the bush."

"He's a friend of yours?"

"Not anymore. He was interested in me. We were lovers, but a long time ago. I don't bother with men now. He was really in love with me. But he's a fucking fool. He still carries the torch. I know it."

"Why didn't it work?"

"I don't know. I treated him bad. I let him pour out his heart and then I left him." She'd shrugged. "I'm bad." Then, running a finger across my lips, she'd said, "Fuck him. Who needs him when I have you?"

I smiled at Apryl in the mirror. "I don't take drugs. Never have," I said. "I'm glad you quit."

"That's good. That's real good. Jeep makes herbal potions, but that's something different altogether. They're for getting rid of demons and shit like that."

I tried to apply my eyeliner, but my hands were shaking and I clasped them together in my lap. I was exhausted. Dorae and I were also having problems with our sex life, although I didn't know exactly what was happening, except that she blamed me for her dissatisfaction and demanded that I think of new things. Every time I tried to bring something creative to our sex life or tried to please her in a way that she wanted, though, she would say that it wasn't right. The memory of a previous night floated through my mind.

Dorae had been lying on top of me and had sighed with exasperation. "I don't like the way you kiss," she'd said. "I don't want to kiss you on the mouth anymore. This is fucking bullshit. I don't want to teach someone to kiss."

"No one complained about my kissing before," I'd objected.

"Yeah? Well, they probably were just as terrible," she'd said. "I'm going to fantasize. When I'm not satisfied, I'm like a man, you know? Maybe I'll just take a cold shower later." She laid her head against my chest and pushed my hands away irritably when I tried to touch her. "Let's just sleep, okay? I'm really disappointed in you."

Agony and confusion overwhelmed me and I shut my eyes tightly to numb out the pain. If only I could put myself in another place, a happier time. I tried vainly to concentrate on a happy memory. Numb out, numb out, I told myself. Tears began to slide silently down my face and I fought back the hysteria rising inside me so that it would not shudder through my body and make itself known. It was hard to breathe. I wanted to sob. Dorae grabbed my hand and brought it to her lips. "Don't cry," she whispered.

"Why not?" I wailed. The tears came harder now. Crying felt good. The pain was washing over me like waves of darkness. "Why not?"

"Because I'm fucked up, that's why. Don't let me fuck you up, too."

"But we can work on it. Everything will be okay."

Dorae rubbed my hand softly, soothingly. She took each finger into her mouth. "In the summer we'll go to California and everything will be okay," she whispered. She was rubbing my breasts through my blouse, lightly tracing the nipples with her fingertips. "Everything will be okay," she whispered, and waves of heat and arousal began to envelop and awaken my body. I knew that we would never go to California, but it did not seem to matter.

"In the summer we'll go to California and everything will be okay," I repeated. My teeth were chattering. I vaguely realized that I was hysterical but the knowledge was only a dull throb in my subconscious. The tears continued to flow like blood from an open wound. "And y-you d-do care about me, don't you, Dorae?"

"Yes, baby. I care about you."

I'd smiled. I knew it was foolish, but a happiness began to radiate through me, soothing me. "Tell me you care. Tell me again and again."

Now I looked at my pale reflection in the Blue Angel's mirror. "Yeah, it's good to get rid of demons. Sometimes I almost feel like taking drugs, just for a night, so I wouldn't feel so anxious."

"For real?" Apryl's eyes were wide. "Cuz if you ever wanted coke, I know where you could get some. Good quality."

◆◆◆◆

A piece of paper protruded from *The Wizard of Oz,* which lay in a drawer at the boardinghouse where Dorae had stuck it. She had been very distant and nervous lately, and guiltily, I picked the paper out to see if she were practicing poetry as she had said on occasion. My hands trembled as I unfolded the piece of paper. There was a film over my eyes as if I was in the middle of a dream. A sharp pain began in my chest. It was a love letter to a man. I had never known that Dorae was capable of passion; she had never shown it with me. With a feeling of unreality pounding like a drum inside my mind, I noticed that the words were taken from love letters I had given to Dorae over the months. Fury mixed with anguish came over me and I was only vaguely aware of the door opening and Dorae's hurried footsteps as she attempted to snatch the letter from me. Her face was white with panic. "What are you doing with that?" she hissed.

"These are my words," I screamed, and I was angry to hear the hysteria in my voice. Hysteria seemed to be always brimming beneath the surface, waiting to arise like a startled bird at the slightest provocation. "You stole my words for some fucking bastard."

"Yes, I used your words," screamed Dorae. "You know how to write beautiful words and I wanted to feel like I could write them, too, for the first time in my life. That letter isn't meant for anyone. It's for a fantasy lover who doesn't exist."

"It's for a fucking guy. Maybe it's for that fucking guy who runs fucking tours—"

"That's not true. You don't know anything. I always wanted you to help me to write and you said you would, but you're all talk." She was panting with fury. "All right then, I won't use your words. I'm not a good writer. Besides, I wasn't stealing your words. I was just borrowing them—"

"I make my living from words! They're my life! You can't borrow them!" I shot back.

"I'll never be a writer! You can have your damn words back!" Her voice rose to a hysterical peak as she tore the letter into bits.

I gathered the bits up, hands trembling, but she pulled me away. "Don't touch them. They don't belong to you—"

I was jittery and confused. "I thought the letter was—"

"Well, you're wrong."

"I'll help you to write, but you can't use my words." I watched as she gathered the pieces of the letter up and shoved them into her bag. I grabbed the purse then and snatched the bits in my hand, spilling the purse's contents, recognizing one of my lipsticks. Dorae grabbed me by my hair and arm, but halfheartedly, and threw me on the bed. She shook me until my teeth rattled. Then she began to throw things around the room, emptying drawers and dashing perfume bottles from the top of the dresser. The hysteria was washing over me, blackening my mind like a thick film, and I hid my face in my hands. This was not my room and it was going to be destroyed. I was going to be destroyed also, because I had loved Dorae, all because I loved her. I was sobbing now, hardly believing the anguish pouring out of me, taking over my body as if I no longer had control of anything at all in my life. The shaking would not stop. The hysteria would not stop. If only the floor would open and I would fall down the long black hole into Wonderland, away from life, away from my broken life. Dorae had pulled me around and was lying on top of me now. She was kissing my face and I was surprised to see that her own face was wet with tears. Her bottom lip was quivering and thick tears fell from her eyes, hitting my face like shattered diamonds. "You bitch. Why do you make me do these things?" she sobbed. "You know I don't want to hurt you, Cynthia. You're a sweet girl. But I don't know how to love you. I never knew how to love anyone! I don't trust anybody, Cynthia. You don't understand—"

"No, no," I said. "I want to understand. Just tell me, please, just talk to me and we'll work it out."

"We're from different worlds, baby, different worlds. Sometimes I think you want to see the darker side of me—" Dorae's voice was hoarse and broken.

"No. I love you. I just want to understand," I pleaded, brushing her tangled gold curls and the endless stream of tears from her wet face. I felt sorrier then for Dorae in her anguished confusion than I did for myself. She told me of her experience in foster homes where her foster parents would hit the children and tell them they were not *their* children. They were never kissed, never held. They hated each other. And when she ran away as a teenager, she was approached by many pimps and there was any number of ways she could have ended up, but she was determined not to be a prostitute and then Dennis came along and her promise as a dancer was discovered and nurtured. But she'd had to fight to survive, it was a fight all the way.

"I'm fucked up, Cynthia. My life's as fucked up as this room, but I'm trying to put the pieces together. That's why I'm a vegetarian. That's why I want to read."

I held her close to me and stroked her head like a baby's. My body was sagging with exhaustion, but never had I felt such intimacy with her as in that moment. Warmth radiated through me, through my exhaustion and trembling body, the burning fever of total abandonment. "You're going to be fine. You have me now. I'll take care of you."

"That's what I'm afraid of! I think you need someone more than me!" Dorae laughed, her eyes red and swollen, but twinkling.

Then we quietly put back the things in the room, cleaning up the perfume bottles that had shattered and laughing about the pungent aromas left on the rug, and we calmly had dinner together, holding hands silently through the meal. Then we sat in a hot bath like two sisters, our legs intertwined, our faces lit by smiles; and the room was cloaked in darkness, with only the soft light from candles that bobbed perilously in candle-holders on the water, casting wild, elongated shadows on the walls. "I think we're both crazy," I giggled.

Dorae sighed with sensual contentment. "I like the way you look," she purred. "All pink and white, healthy. Promise me you won't worry about anything. I don't want you getting old and wrinkled on me before your time."

I rubbed my foot along her glistening leg. "I won't."

Then she lifted a sopping wet calf out of the water. "Do y'all think my calves will get as big as yours? I mean, what do y'all think, sugar lamb?"

◆◆◆◆

I was hot under the lamppost on Bourbon Street in my tight peach dress and high pumps. I looked impatiently at my watch. Dorae was supposed to meet me at ten, but she was forever late. Fifteen minutes had lapsed already. I twisted the handle of my purse nervously and crowds of lumbering teenage tourists, cavorting loudly and carrying oversized drinks from the local bars, began to whistle and make inept passes at me. My heavy, layered brown hair was falling in ringlets with the humidity. I was hoping that my makeup would not be evaporating in the heat. I paced impatiently, worriedly. Why the hell was Dorae late on my birthday night? Couldn't she be on time for once? After another half hour, I wandered over to the Ripley Museum, casting backward glances at the corner where we were slated to meet. My heart rose and fell as any number of golden-haired women who might have been Dorae but weren't passed. I made a mental note to do an article on Ripley if I could find the proper market. An hour passed and a fury began to rise up inside of me mixed with pain. "I'm dating a goddamn five-year-old," I thought. Dorae had moved back in with Dennis, the conflicts there seemingly resolved. But she was just as erratic. I was happy that she was now taking English courses at night, although she seemed terribly distressed by them. I dialed Dorae from a phone booth and was surprised and irritated when she answered.

"Why haven't you left yet?" I cried.

Dorae's voice wavered nervously and she was obviously short of breath. "I'm getting ready as quickly as I can," she said. "I had to do some laundry—"

"Laundry!" I cried. "It's practically midnight. Why on earth—"

"Please, no lectures," she said. "You want me to get there, don't you? So I shouldn't be on the phone."

"No, you should be on Bourbon Street, but an hour ago—"

"I'll be there. Okay? Okay?" Her voice sounded pained.

"I'm sorry, baby." I sighed deeply. It was impossible to stay mad at Dorae. The idea of her dashing around her apartment nervously trying to make an appointment that anyone else would have made on time touched me. She was a child. A little girl trapped in a gorgeous woman's body.

A street mime with a white, bejeweled face and a clown's acrobatic ability began to make exaggerated eyes at me and fan himself with feigned ardor as I giggled. He was trying to catch an invisible butterfly with an invisible net. I immersed myself in our rapport for an indefinite time until I looked at my watch and saw that another hour had elapsed. I began to shiver, even though it was hot and muggy in the Quarter. The mime sensed my unhappiness and began to point to the corners of his painted mouth, imitating my glumness. I forced a smile, but the pit of my stomach was beginning to churn. When another hour had lapsed, I knew she was not coming. My anger changed to waves of panic as I wondered if there had been some sort of terrible accident. I called her house again, hands shaking, hysteria rising in me.

"Dorae left an hour ago," Dennis told me.

"What?" My voice was a shriek. The street seemed to rise and buck before me. "She was supposed to meet me here at Bourbon Street for my birthday."

"Poor, dear Cynthia." Dennis sighed. "Is that so? Well, Dorae said that she was going to meet you, but I knew it wasn't true. She's been moving out her things bit by bit for weeks now."

"Moving? Moving where?" The nightmare was spreading through my mind like ink on a napkin.

"She left to live with her boyfriend, that fucker she's with—"

"Boyfriend? What are you talking about?! I'm her lover! Can't you acknowledge that?! She said she doesn't deal with men anymore — she's spent every minute with me—"

"Poor, dear Cynthia. Dorae doesn't mean any harm. She sees someone and she's attracted to them. And people are drawn to her like bees to honey. Men and women both. Lots of them. It never lasts. She doesn't mean to hurt anyone. She's just a flopsy girl — and now this new guy came along. She wanted me to explain it to you. She's a coward. She really likes you—"

"Why didn't she talk to me?" I was screaming. My nerves were jangling and pain stabbed at the pit of my stomach like a knife.

"She's a flopsy girl. She called me to ask me to talk to you. She doesn't want to hurt you, but she couldn't face you — she liked you. I'm sure she even loved you. She really did. But she runs away. He won't last. They never do."

"What?!"

"How do you think I feel? Do you know who I am?"

"H-her father."

"I'm her lover, too. There hasn't been much for me these past few years, but I've had her for a lot longer than you — and now she's left me."

"Fuck you! She was twelve years old! You abused her! She's not going to do this to me!"

"Don't talk this way. She's just a troubled girl; she means no harm. I'd have to protect her if you're planning to hurt her—"

"Fuck you!" I slammed down the phone. That night I walked endlessly without seeing, trying to outdistance my thoughts. I felt shattered, broken by my grief. My teeth were chattering; the tears seemed like they would never stop flowing, never soothe. I was blind with rage: I didn't know if I could survive without Dorae. My mind arranged wild scenarios in my grief, sometimes violent. I wanted to hurt the bastards who had hurt me. No one could do this to me. I wouldn't let them. I thought I'd die from the pain.

The manager of the Blue Angel told me that Dorae had quit and joined an accounting firm. I would find her. She could not run from me as she'd run all her life.

Like a woman possessed, hands shaking, all the nerves in my body jumping, I began calling all the accounting firms in New Orleans asking about a new employee. On the third try, I found my answer. I had all the time in the world as I waited outside that office building, my senses heightened in my anxiety and pain, looking wild and disoriented to passersby and even to that objective corner of myself that observed the whole spectacle with calm bemusement. Finally she came to the building, apparently finished with lunch, stopping when she saw me to gasp, "Cynthia? What are you doing here?!" Her face was ashen and her eyes, like mine, had the dark shadows under them of someone suffering from a long illness. I was happy to see at least that.

"You can't get away with this," I said through my teeth. I was quivering in every pore of my body, but my rage dissolved the instant I saw her. She was the Dorae I loved and I could never hurt her. She was helpless, and her face, with its wide black eyes, was taut with anxiety and childlike confusion as she assessed the situation before her, my poor lost baby who always had to fight to survive, who was as frightened and innocent as a caged animal even now. It hurt me to see her fear of me.

"What do you want from me?! What do you want?!" she shrieked.

"I don't know," I said emptily.

That night we met and argued and said nasty words but then we were hugging and running to the Mississippi River to watch the boats together. Nothing seemed to matter again but that we were together.

Dorae put her head on my shoulder and said, "Don't think I don't feel bad about things. But, Cynthia, he's going to help me. He knows a lot about herbs. He takes good care of me."

There was a dull pain inside me to hear this other person, this *man,* acknowledged. "What about me?! Didn't I take care of you?! *I* love you! No one could love you more than me!"

"I know, baby. It doesn't make sense to you — I don't make sense to *me* either. I'm fucked up, that's all. I couldn't go on living with Dennis. I couldn't tell you about him because I was afraid I'd lose that thing in you I liked." Dorae hugged me. "Oh, God, I'm so confused. I still care about you, you bitch. I love you. And we will always be friends. I don't know if you'd want to be my friend—"

"Of course I will."

I looked at Dorae, magnificent under the lights from the Promenade, effortlessly beautiful with her satin-smooth skin and lush face, like a photograph that burned its image into your mind forever, and felt I could never love anyone as much as her. And her upper lip curled with sensual abandon, her black eyes beautiful and smoky and clear like a child's.

Like true lovers, we watched the stars. Inside I felt broken, but I held Dorae again as if I would never let go and determined to believe that we would be together ultimately against all the odds, that the illusion would never be shattered.

The pain and anger would continue to erupt like a poison leaving the body. I would return to New York to re-establish my shattered career, and at first I would fly often to New Orleans to be with Dorae, obsessed by the idea that we would be together, that nothing could stand in the way of our love. There would always be new lovers and we'd argue and live out dramatic scenes and then take hot baths together like the best of friends, with the candles burning and the lights dim. And sometimes we would make love again against mirrors on the tiles and I would feel an aching, overwhelming love and sadness and dream that we would marry, although it would never happen.

As time went on, the torrid, passionate friendship became less frantic, and we saw each other less and less. One day we argued about a circus and never saw each other again. Dorae went to a holistic retreat in Massachusetts with a fresh-faced blonde named Epiphany. She left no forwarding address or number, although she did call twice to say that she was doing well and that there would always be something between us. I felt released and new and was glad the relationship was over, although I still said, "I love you," to Dorae on the phone and felt it deep inside like an old friend.

But at that moment by the Mississippi River, the night felt as if it could surely be suspended into eternity, because I was with Dorae and the greatness of our love and desire kept us very alive in the moment. One large star was burning brightly and beautifully over the Mississippi, adrift in the night. It was as fragile and beautiful as my poor, lost Dorae and very alone, but its long rays still burned on, searching and searching before daylight, like a lost heart. I hoped it would find the way.

A letter of apology to Ms. Alice

++++   *Dorothy Love*

Dear Ms. Alice,
   I jest found out somebody been writing you letters
in my name. Honest, Ms. Alice, I never said none o' that stuff.
I don't goes round messing wit womens like you. I has my own
place and I knows that nobody like me is gonna even dream ...
Well, Ms. Alice, I hope you do understand what I trying to say
here. When yo cousin Dede told me you was talking bout some
stuff in some kind o' letter you thought was from me, her best
friend, why, you shoulda seen my broke face cause I know —
and this the God truth — I ain't writ you no letter or nothing.
I always respectful to other womens and try and treat everybody nice and everything, but Lordy, I wouldn't never say none
o' that stuff to nobody. Least o' all nobody like you, a eduacated
writer woman. I mean what you want to hear a whole lotta
trashmouth talk bout womens loving other womens for? And
what I know bout som'in like that? Nothin, that's what. I don't
know nothing bout no womens loving on womens period.
   'Cept that one time when we was at that fish fry over in
Fairfield and Delton Ivers come sliding up to me and tells me
to come round to the shed wit him in the back. Now everybody knowed Delton was kinda That Way? So I musta looked

at him like he was Crazy's mama cause he just turn up his little pouty mouth and say he wanted to *show* me something. So I went on wit him and sure nough, there was som'in to see. It was Enolia Glass and that manwoman Jessie Agnes.

Jessie Agnes was on top o' Enolia jest like a man. Had her skirt heitched up round her neck and she was jest a pumping like it the most natu'al thing in the world. Won't no way they was go know me and Delton standing there watching cause they was back up in the coner on a stack o' old scratchy blankets thowed cross John Glass' — that's Enolia's daddy — workbench. So we watched the whole thing. Jessie Agnes, she always wo britches, had tooken off her pants and didn't have a stitch on under that. She had Enolia's bloomers off, too. Lord, I never seen nothing like it.

They was making noises too. Not being quiet as they coulda been, probly like they shoulda been, cause that's what put nosey Delton on to 'em. Jessie Agnes starts asking Enolia did she like it. And Enolia says I likes it, Baby, I always likes it. It always good to me. Then she starts to whimper like a little sick puppy. Jessie Agnes had one hand under Enolia's romp, the other one squeezing her tiddy and she was pushing herself up into Enolia, in and out hard. Moon bright enough to see everything.

Enolia reaches over Jessie Agnes' back and starts scratching like a cat and she moving and wiggling under Jessie Agnes like ain't no tomorrow. We hear her say aw fuck me bulldagger, fuck me bulldagger, and Bulldagger fucks her. Enolia throws her head back and let it hang over the table. She just about outa her mind now. Jessie Agnes musta done som'in wit that hand under her booty, cause Enolia started sounding like she gon cry and jumping mo like a fish laying up on that table than a girl.

Then they put theyselves better to each other. Enolia puts her hands on her own pussy and holds it open for Jessie Agnes. Now I knows what a woman got and what she ain't got. I'm a woman; my mama one; and I got three sisters, all womens. So I knows ain't no woman got no thing down there. But I guess Jessie Agnes ain't no woman, no natu'al one anyway. Cause she got *some'in* down there. I didn't see *it* but I saw her fix herself to put it in Enolia's pussy. And when she do that, Enolia starts cooing real low and gravley. All the time Jessie Agnes jest stroking away. (Well, that all you can call it, even if it is womens.) She keeps her little tight ass in a tight little swirl pushing and mashing that thing she got into Enolia's pussy.

Enolia still groaning. It getting real good to her now. She starts flicking her tongue everywhere, biting and licking on Jessie Agnes. Jessie Agnes grabs Enolia's thighs and pushes 'em way back over her head, puts her hands down there again, and they go it some more. Then I hear Enolia start to come. She crying and hollering, Jessie crying too. Well, damn, I says to Delton, they both coming together. Enolia's hips start rising to the ceiling like som'in pulling her and Jessie up off the table. Jessie gets faster and harder, then she gets real slow and push back off her hands and catches her arms round Enolia's thigh joints.

Then they come. The more Enolia comes the crazier Jessie Agnes gets and comes and hollers. And they both jest shaking like they in a earthquake. Then when you figure they all don for, Enolia reaches down and sticks her finger up Jessie Agnes' asshole and draws it back up her crack real slow. Jessie Agnes hollers like the last lifeblood leaving her. Then they both be still.

I jest looks at Delton and he looks at me. When we back in the house, he pleased wit hisself cause he made me see som'in and now I can't go round messing wit him bout his being the only one funny anymore. Delton made me promise I wouldn't tell it to nobody. And I didn't . Not even Dede. And I just told you but you not in Fairfield, so that's alright. Anyway, the only reason I brung it up was to say that's the onliest thing I ever did wit womens was to watch Enolia and Jessie Agnes that time. I wouldn't know to do nothing myself and I ain't thought that much about it in the first place. So I know I ain't go write no love letter to no writer lady and say a whole bunch o' trashy stuff. You know, I bet Delton did that. It jest like him cause I told him how when Dede bought your book, we slept in one big bed one night — you, me, and Dede while she read it to me. And he start asking me after that bout doing it wit womens and when I told him he think cause *he* funny everybody is but you a nice woman and a writer and me and Dede sho ain't never don it he say I ain't been seen wit no mens lately and me and Dede sure thick enough so maybe us like womens, too.

Well, even if it was Delton who wrote you, I know he don't mean harm and just fooling wit me so don't take it bad. B'lieve me, Ms. Alice, me and Dede ain't doing nothing like that. I jest don't have time for boys anymore, that's all. I'm trying to finish night school and tending that cafe in the daytime plus help raise two lil sisters at the same time, so when I got time for anything else, mens, womens, chilren, dogs, nothing? Dede my best friend so she the one I talk to bout things. But she knows I ain't sent you no love letter though. So I hope you straight now.

Well, I has to go. I didn't mean to take up so much yo time. I know you must be very busy. If you feel it though, you can write me. I hope you doing good. We sho' look forward to reading yo next book. Take care yourself, hear. Bye for now.

Yours truly,
Annie

Sweat

✦✦✦✦   *Catherine Houser*

"Why am I doing this?" Ana's left leg flailed through the air in a halfhearted kick that would have made the Rockettes cringe.

"Kick those legs, ladies — and-one-and-two-and-three-and-four — let's go, girls — flabby thighs don't attract bedroom eyes."

"That's it. I'm outta here," Ana mumbled to herself as she bent down and picked up her damp towel and retreated from the big pink-and-blue room full of bouncing women in day-glo spandex. Outside the aerobics room, Ana leaned against the wall of mirrors and let her sweaty body slide down to the ground, leaving a glistening trail of sweat behind. There were women everywhere — some pedaling the stationary bikes, some struggling to keep pace on the stair machines, and a few working the weight machines. Women, women everywhere and not another dyke to be found.

Ana buried her face in her towel, soaking up the sweat that rolled down her face like tears. "What am I doing here?" she mumbled to herself. "I couldn't find a date here if I stripped naked and hung out a 'For Rent' sign." She wiped her face vigorously as if trying to wipe away the reality that she was the only lesbian in a gym full of perfectly straight women. When she looked up again her eyes focused on a tanned, sinewy leg flexing and stretching just in front of her. Ana's gaze languished on the smooth, taut skin for a moment, then followed the supple muscle line up past the knee to the short-cut black bicycle pants and the apple ass that filled them. From the back, the woman stretching out in front of Ana reminded her of herself before five years of computer hacking had taken its toll on her widening hips and burgeoning belly. That was really why she was here in this gym in the first place — to get that body back. Getting her first date in two years was secondary to the ultimate hard body — at least that's what she told herself every day as motivation for coming back to the gym. The woman in front of her rolled over onto her back and began doing leg lifts to some internal rhythm. Her hips rocked back and forth with the force of her flexed legs, and her undulating abdomen, which lay free and inviting between the top of her pants and the bottom of her black spandex halter, was dewy with perspiration. Ana, lost in those rhythmic hips and legs, began counting quietly to herself as if keeping pace for the woman stretched out in front of her, and when the woman rolled over onto all fours and began kicking one leg out in back of her, Ana didn't miss a beat. With each straight-back thrust of her leg, the woman brought her head forward and up, arching so that Ana could see the veins in her neck bulge with exertion, then snapping her head back down to almost touch her now-bent knee. Ana watched the woman's curly black hair bob with the motion of her body. She watched as sweat rolled down her strained neck muscles and she imagined herself lying under her, the object of so much effort.

"No. No straight women," Ana said, bopping herself in the head with her wet towel.

"Excuse me?" the woman in black turned and asked Ana, not missing a beat in her leg kick routine.

"Oh, nothing, just mumbling to myself." Embarrassed, Ana got up and headed for the locker room, hoping to sweat out some of her frustration in the sauna.

Ana always worked hard in the gym, alternating between lifting weights and working out on a stair machine, and even taking a few aerobic classes when she felt she wouldn't gag on the Mary Sunshine attitude of the instructor. Finally, after three months, she was beginning to feel some results. Alone in the low light of the sauna, Ana sat on the cedar bench and ran her hands the length of her legs, tracing the outline of muscle and bone. Then she reached up and cradled her pendulous breasts through the thin white towel, gently nudging them up to where they used to be. "After thirty, everything heads south." Ana closed her eyes and saw herself in years past fielding a hard-hit grounder at short stop and going for the double play. She saw the curves and lines of a healthy, firm body, her body before the cancer sent her into hiding in oversized sweats. Through the terrycloth, she fingered the walnut-sized hollow in her left breast. "One year, three months, and twelve days." Her face stretched up to the light as if it were the sun providing this desert heat. So lost was she in a survivor's ascent into heat and light that she didn't hear the door close beside her.

"Do that a lot, do you?"

Startled, Ana jumped, clutched her towel to her chest, and fumbled to refasten it more tightly around her.

"I'm sorry, I didn't mean to scare you."

Ana looked up and found herself eye to eye with the woman she had been watching stretch and kick on the gym floor. The wet curls of black hair framed searing blue eyes and an all-too-flashy perfect smile.

"No, no, you didn't scare me. I was just spacing out. It gets so hot in here I think it does funny things to your brain." Ana tried to laugh off her embarrassment and politely moved to the side to make room for the dark-haired woman on the lower bench.

"No, that's okay. You're fine where you are. I go for the hot spot," she said, climbing up to the top bench, where the sauna heat felt like jet exhaust. Despite the signs posted throughout the locker room imploring, "No nudity," and, "Swimwear must be worn in sauna, steam room, and jacuzzi," the dark-haired woman undid her pink towel, exposing an evenly tanned body. Ana closed her eyes and breathed deeply, fighting the urge to let her eyes linger on the sight. "God, I love it in here. Reminds me of home."

"Home? No place on earth is as hot as this," Ana said.

"Apparently you haven't been in the Arizona desert in July — one degree north of hell."

"Arizona? Is that where you're from?" Trying not to look, or at least not to stare, Ana kept sneaking glimpses of the naked woman sitting above, facing her.

"Yep."

"What the hell are you doing in Vermont in February?"

"Work. I'm an itinerant teacher of sorts. I do a semester here, a semester there. This year it was Smith and the University of Vermont. But come May, I'll be back in the desert heat for real."

"What do you teach?"

"Creative writing," the woman said, as if the two words were an oxymoron.

Ana was suddenly enveloped by the smell of oranges. She looked up to see the woman breaking apart a newly peeled one.

"Would you like some?" she said, dangling a dripping slice of the orange from the end of a sweat-shimmering arm. "By the way, my name is Liz."

Ana, intrigued at how easily this woman lived in her skin, reached up and accepted the fleshy piece of fruit, licking at the juice dripping from it before putting the whole piece in her mouth. She chewed quickly and swallowed hard, surprised by her own hunger and thirst.

"I'm Ana."

"And what do you do, Ana?" Liz spoke between licking and nibbling at pieces of orange.

"I'm a systems analyst. I spend most of my day sitting in front of a computer — which is why I'm here — trying to work something more than my brain and my fingers." Ana reached up and began kneading her shoulders. "The stress gets to me sometimes." Ana dropped her head and worked the muscle across one shoulder and down her back as far as she could reach.

Liz put down the rest of her orange, wiped her hands on her towel, and said, "Here, let me help with that. The parts that need it the most are the ones you can't reach."

Ana looked up and shook her head. "No, that's okay."

"Are you sure? You know, between the itinerant parts of my life, I run a massage practice in Tucson. This is your chance at a freebie," Liz said, stretching her hands, bending her fingers back and forth as though she were getting ready to play a concerto.

"Seriously? God, I've been searching for a good massage therapist for months." Ana thought of her many trials during the time she was dealing with the stress of the cancer diagnosis. Despite her pleas, no one she ever went to worked deeply enough, pressed hard enough, got to the life energy held tightly deep in her tissues. She watched Liz press her fingers against the cedar wall and followed the lines of sweat and muscle up one arm, across her shoulder, and down to a flawless breast that gently rose and fell with each contraction of her pectorals. A lightning bolt of lust shot through her genitals only to rise back up and settle in her belly as fear. "No, really, it's okay."

"Yeah, I know, but I can make it better." Liz beckoned with her hands, moved to the edge of the bench, and opened her legs. "Come on — I won't bite — unless you ask me to."

A flush of red exploded across Ana's chest as she looked up to see Liz brush wet raven curls from her forehead. She couldn't read this woman. Liz seemed so comfortable in her body, as if she were really in there inhabiting and owning every cell of her being instead of floating outside it judging it as others might see it. Ana imagined herself naked in front of this rakish woman and found herself fumbling with her towel, retucking the end of it securely just above her left breast. "Not on your life," Ana mumbled into her own chest.

"You're doing it again."

"What?"

"Mumbling to yourself. Better watch out, someone with good hearing might be eavesdropping." And with that Liz stretched gracefully down the length of the bench and around the corner and sat behind Ana, framing her with a glistening leg alongside each arm. Then her hands were on her like tropical rain, wet and warm. Liz's strong hands spanned Ana's neck, alternately cupping and smoothing the long muscles across her shoulders and running her lusciously padded fingertips up the steely muscles to the base of Ana's head. Their sweat mingled, providing a natural lubricant that allowed Liz's hands to move across Ana's skin like a wet tongue on melting ice. Ana gave herself over to them. "That's it. Let it all go." Liz's breath, cool and fruity, settled over her but did nothing to quell the fire sparking in her genitals and rising into her chest.

What if she's straight? Ana thought, careful not to give the words voice. *Worse, what if she's not?* Ana hadn't been with anyone since before the surgery, before the drugs, before disease gripped her body. It had taken her months of standing naked in front of mirrors, of watching herself move, of touching and caressing herself before she was able to see her body not so much as an enemy, a traitor, but as an ally, a friend even. Working out was just another step on that road. As much as she longed for the intimate touch of another woman, she wasn't sure she was ready. "Still too brittle. Too breakable," she said.

"We're working on that," Liz said as she worked her way down under the towel stretched tight across the middle of

Ana's back. Ana's creamy skin was cool and damp where the towel had clung and Liz's fingers were like hot pulsating water running down her back. So lost was Ana in those hands and her own thoughts that she didn't realize she'd spoken or that Liz had replied until there was a gentle tug at the towel and Liz's lips were at her ear saying, "Come on, it's awfully hard to work around this towel."

Ana clutched at the towel in front, trying to hold the ends together. "What if someone comes in?"

Liz grabbed her water bottle and her own pink towel, jumped up, and headed for the door. Ana's heart sank. Had she lost her chance to find out who this woman was, who *she* was? But Liz stopped at the door, wedged her water bottle into the handle to block anyone from opening the door from the outside, and then draped her towel over the small window on the door.

"There. They'll think it's broken. Besides, no straight women need apply."

Ana looked at Liz as she stood facing her, naked and glistening with sweat, arms akimbo, the pale yellow light haloing a mop of wet black curls and highlighting those playful blue eyes. She looked as though she'd just conquered her piece of the world.

"See, you'd best be careful about those little conversations you have with yourself. Next to eye contact, lesbians are known for their keen sense of hearing." Liz moved toward her, gently directing her to lie on her belly on the bench. "Come on, I want to work that lower back. Actually, I think we're known for our keen senses, period. Every last one of them, and a few they haven't discovered yet."

Ana was mesmerized by Liz's enthusiasm and was beginning to feel a bit like Liz's prey as she awkwardly maneuvered herself onto her belly, still holding the towel together in front. Liz's hand rested tenderly on the back of Ana's head, her fingers lightly stroking Ana's straight, short-cropped, blondish brown hair. Ana was comforted by her soft, lingering touch.

"That's okay. Keep the towel if it makes you feel more comfortable." Liz's voice was lower, less buoyant. "I want to help you relax, not make you more tense. Do you mind if I just work with my hands under the towel? I don't want to irritate your skin by moving a damp towel across it."

"That's fine."

Liz spread Ana's legs apart and kneeled between them. She reached up under the towel and Ana immediately felt the heat from her hands on her buttocks, even though Liz's hands only hovered above them on the way up her back. The heels of Liz's hands settled alongside Ana's spine and pressed deeply into the muscles there. Ana felt dozens of little electric currents shoot from Liz's hands, through those muscles and out the front of her. With each repositioned press of Liz's hands into Ana's back she felt an electrical storm blow through her body. She could see now, in the distance against a field of midnight blue, bolts of lightning, white and hot, igniting the sky. Her body began to let go, to expand, to be the tableau for those lightning flashes.

"This is where fear lives," Liz said as she worked her way up and down Ana's lower back.

"Hand him an eviction notice."

Liz laughed out loud and Ana could feel the laughter in her hands as they danced across her back, smoothing her wet skin. "Clever, very clever." Liz bent down so that her head hovered just above the towel and said in a low, deep voice, "Out, damn fear, out."

Ana's giggle grew to a full-bellied laugh that exploded from her body.

"Ssshh. Someone will hear us."

The two giggled and laughed even harder as they tried to control themselves. Trying to calm herself, Ana pulled her legs in. Now her inner thighs hugged Liz's bent legs as she kneeled between them. Ana soaked in the sweaty warmth of Liz's powerful legs, imagining the taste and texture of the skin at the back of those knees. She drew her thighs tighter, wanting to wrap herself around them. And then, as if by reflex, as Liz, still trying to calm her giggles, worked her back, Ana bent her legs until her heels met Liz's naked back, and brought Liz facedown, squarely against her back. She pinned her there for a moment, holding her tightly with her legs. Liz wiggled her hands down from Ana's back, tracing the curves of Ana's waist and hips.

"Interesting move." Liz breathed the words into Ana's neck, where earlier she'd loosened the taut muscles. The sound, so close, so intimate, vibrated down Ana's spine, out to the tips of her fingers, and returned in waves of desire. Ana wanted this woman, wanted to wrap herself around Liz and take her inside, swallow her whole. But panic quelled her hunger as Liz's open lips moved across Ana's shoulders and her hands swept up and down her sides, loosening the towel with each pass. Ana suddenly wanted to be invisible. The fear of being seen as weak, as diseased, as less than whole, was so potent that it drained the passion from her like sweat. Ana let loose of Liz with her legs and squirmed out from under her. Liz let her up and sat watching as Ana collected herself, pulling the towel tightly together again and smoothing her hair back from her forehead.

"What's the matter? Did I do something wrong?" Liz's eyes flashed transparent as an inviting vulnerability moved across her face.

"No, it's not you. It's me." Ana lowered her head, wondering how to excuse herself gracefully, while longing for the strength not to have to.

Liz raised her hand and lightly touched Ana's cheek, a single fingertip tracing a line of sweat rolling from her temple to her chin. "What are you afraid of?"

"You. Me. Everything." Ana's eyes met Liz's, her face unconsciously moving toward Liz's hand like a kitten arching to meet it. Ana suddenly felt tired, exhausted from her workout and the heat of the sauna and from the battle raging inside her between her need for love and her need to stay safe. Too tired to fight anymore, she laid her head against Liz's shoulder, nuzzling her face into the wet hollow at the base of Liz's neckline. Ana watched Liz's gleaming breasts rise and fall with each deep breath and she wanted them, wanted to take them in her mouth, wanted her tongue and lips and face and hands to know every perfect inch of them.

"You don't have to be afraid of me. I don't want you to do anything you don't want to." Liz cradled her with one arm, one hand resting tenderly on Ana's shoulder while her other smoothed Ana's hair away from her face. Buoyed by Liz's solid arms and the salty smell of her sweat, Ana floated for a moment in a sea in which passion rose in ever-burgeoning waves cresting in white flashes of fear. Using visualization techniques she'd learned in her healing, Ana pictured the swells of desire rolling over the fear, consuming it. Ana's hand ascended to caress Liz's breast and her face slid down to meet it there. Ana's tongue swept across Liz's slick, hot breast until it found a purple, engorged nipple. Liz arched to meet Ana's flicking tongue; Ana met Liz's desire with her own, covering as much skin as she could with her mouth, licking and sucking. Liz held her there for a long moment, arching and sighing deeply, then she lifted Ana's face and engaged her in a long, luscious union of tongues and lips that lifted Ana off the bench so that she was standing in front of Liz, between her legs, bending over her, exploring the corners of her mouth with her tongue. Liz sat with her head bent back and up, her mouth following Ana's lead, her hand resting lightly on the towel clinging to Ana's hips.

Startled by the sound of someone at the door, Ana jumped back. Both of the women stared at the door, watching to see if the water bottle would stay wedged in its place. From the hallway they heard people complaining about the sauna being "broken again."

Liz winked and they both giggled quietly at their ingenuity. "Now, as long as we don't spontaneously combust in here we'll be okay."

"We'll be okay," Ana said as she flipped off the heat via the timer and took her place again standing between Liz's legs. She drank in Liz's blue eyes and felt waves of lust well up in her chest and genitals. Ana closed her eyes, breathed in the briny odor of the sauna, and again saw waves of blue overtaking whitecaps of fear. Her eyes still shut tightly, she reached for the corner of the towel tucked over her left breast, plucked it free, and let the towel fall to the ground. Like a child playing peek-a-boo, she kept her eyes closed for a moment, hoping not to be seen.

"Ah, the hidden treasures. Stunning. Absolutely stunning," Liz said. She watched a scarlet flush sweep down from Ana's neck across her round, full breasts and settle in the ragged, raw-looking scar on her left breast. She reached for Ana but stopped short of touch, awaiting an invitation. Liz wasn't sure whether it was a tear or a line of sweat that rolled down the outer line of Ana's cheek to the corner of her mouth.

Ana peeked out from under long, curled lashes, searching for her reflection in Liz's eyes. Her knees went weak when she found desire there instead of the pity she'd feared. Liz slid her hand around Ana's sweat-slick hips to cup her buttocks and pulled Ana toward her into her open mouth. She traveled the full terrain of Ana's silken belly with her lips and tongue, leaving a trail of small wet kisses along her rib bones as she made her way slowly up to nuzzle Ana's breast. She felt Ana snatch a quick breath and hold it as if she were suddenly afraid of drowning. She rested the full of her face against the outside of Ana's breast, her eyelashes fluttering at the edge of the scar like a butterfly. Ana floated for a moment in the powerful embrace of this gentle woman lover, then a sly smile lifted the corners of her mouth and she gave herself over to her.

Ana moved deeper in between Liz's legs while she directed Liz's mouth to her throbbing breast. Liz's mouth, eager but restrained, welcomed the firm nipple, but only after delicately kissing her way around the full circumference of the reddened hollow just above it. Wet, sucking sounds filled the room as Liz made her way back and forth between and around Ana's aching breasts. In a syncopated rhythm with her mouth, Liz's hands roamed from Ana's buttocks across her taut hamstrings and back again, and with each pass her fingertips ventured deeper between Ana's legs. Ana's knees grew weaker with each teasing touch; she wanted Liz in her so badly that she had to fight the impulse to impale herself on those fleeting fingers. Instead, she rose up and sat straddling Liz's lap, her legs locked around Liz's torso, her creamy wetness mingling with Liz's damp pubic hairs, their mouths trying to consume each other. Ana's hips gyrated in small circular motions against Liz's pubic bone as Liz gripped her buttocks, heightening the pressure. Then, in a dance of tongues and hips, Liz reached up from behind and entered her. First one finger, then another, and finally Ana's vagina swallowed up a third. Ana clutched Liz's shoulders and rode her hand like a spirited wild animal, leaning back and catapulting forward, her breath punctuating the perfect pitch of Liz's sturdy fingers until finally an ecstatic spasm seized Ana's body, expelling Liz's fingers in a flood of creamy delight.

Still panting, and more ravenous than she'd ever imagined possible, Ana slumped into Liz's arms, her open mouth moving across Liz's angular shoulder, her teeth gently nipping at the smooth skin stretched over her clavicle. Liz threw her head back, the long muscles of her neck stretched tight, the blue veins pulsing an invitation. Ana's tongue followed the slick edge of muscle up to Liz's earlobe, where it darted in and around, tantalizing and tickling. Feeling a plucky strength return to her legs, Ana stood and laid Liz down on the cedar planks, then lowered herself onto her, their sweaty shining bodies slipping across each other as if they'd been bathed in oil. Like silk, Ana slid down Liz's bronzed body, leaving a trail of kisses and caresses in her wake. The tip of her tongue dipped into her navel, then circled the outer rim and dipped again as prelude to the teasing to come. Ana's voluptuous lips sandwiched Liz's fine hipbone, following it from its outer edge down to the top of Liz's salty, wet cunt. Ana inhaled the deep sea smells, then let out a low sigh that left hot breath hovering over Liz's throbbing mound. Liz arched in the direction of that heat, trying to make contact with Ana's mouth. Ana's tongue darted between pubic hairs to strike like lightning against Liz's clit, then was gone. Ana made her way down Liz's left leg, meeting muscle with mouth and tongue, until she reached Liz's toes. She took each into her mouth, licking and sucking as if they were premium ice cream. Leaving her left leg wet and satiated, Ana picked up Liz's right foot and licked a line from the arch of her foot up the back of her leg to the creases behind her knee. There she lingered, making love to the back of Liz's knee, coaxing pleasure from each crease and sending orgasmic spasms through the tendons and ligaments up and down both of Liz's legs.

Ana draped Liz's spent legs over her shoulders and lay down so that her breasts nestled against Liz's hot, juicy cunt. She rested her head for a moment on Liz's belly. Liz's fingers aimlessly combed through Ana's wet hair as she slowly began wiggling her hips in search of one of Ana's breasts. Ana picked up on the cue, rose up on her hands, and angled her breast and its stiff nipple across the threshold of Liz's vaginal opening. The pink-tipped nipple teased at the engorged opening as Liz's levitating hips sought out its exquisite pleasure. Holding Liz's weight on her shoulders, Ana let her breast frolick with Liz's cunt in midair for a moment. Then, as if changing partners, Ana moved her mouth to where her breast had been and began slurping and sucking and drinking Liz in. Her tongue traveled the folds from Liz's sweet vagina up to her clit and back again several times before focusing its powers on Liz's swollen clit. The long luscious licks matched the rhythm of Liz's undulating hips, keeping time and making the swift change from long, slow strokes to ever more quick flicks as Liz's passion began to crest in wave after orgasmic wave. Ana gently laid Liz's legs down and slid up to cover Liz's mouth with her own wetness before she collapsed across her.

"You are amazing," Liz said, luxuriously running her hands the length of Ana's back. "So much for turning off the heat in here — I'm parched." Liz lazily reached up to the bench above, searching for what was left of her orange. Using tongue and teeth she pulled off a section, bit into it, and let the juice run down the back of her throat. She pulled off another section and offered it from between her teeth to Ana, who wrapped her lips around the wedge of orange, bit into it to release the juice, and then covered Liz's mouth with a sloppy, orange-filled kiss. With renewed energy, Liz rose to meet Ana's mouth, at the same time rolling Ana over onto her back, their sweaty, slippery bodies sliding breast against breast, belly against wet belly until Liz sat up and positioned herself cross-legged between Ana's legs. She looked up at Ana as she lay stretched out on her back, satisfied. Liz pulled apart another wedge of orange, held it up in front of her, and smiled a wicked smile from behind it. "Hmm, I think I just discovered the perfect topping for an orange." She licked the shiny wedge first, then ran it along Ana's creamy cunt. Ana smiled at the coolness of the fleshy fruit against her clit, raising her hips to meet it before Liz snatched it away and popped it in her mouth. The two giggled at their improvisation, and Liz pulled off another section of orange and licked it as Ana raised her hips again, her clit anticipating the cool, soft fruit. Instead, Liz slipped the fleshy wedge into Ana's wet vagina, quickly following it with her tongue. Ana gripped the orange with firm internal muscles, teasing it away from Liz's pursuing tongue. Liz engaged in the game, licking and sucking at the lips of Ana's vagina, trying to coax the orange out. Ana released it for a moment, letting the tip of it slip out just long enough for Liz to take a quick nibble of it before Ana gripped it again tightly within her vaginal walls. Liz, now ravenous, sought out the sweet fruit as she plunged her tongue into Ana's vagina, exploring its firm, fleshy walls and rolling around the piece of orange. Ana giggled, her small convulsions involuntarily releasing the chunk of orange into Liz's hungry mouth, where it exploded in a fruity, creamy come.

Liz sat up, took Ana's hands, pulled her up so that the two women were facing each other, and wrapped Ana in a powerfully joyous hug. "I'll never look at an orange the same way again." They laughed, wiped the sweat from each other's faces, and leaned against each other as they stood, testing the strength of their legs like newborn fillies. They wavered, holding on to each other, steadying themselves. "It's the heat in here, you know, they always make it too hot," Liz quipped. She bent down and picked up Ana's towel and handed it to her as she brushed her lips across her breast. Ana held the towel in front of her for a moment as Liz turned to take her towel down from the window, pulled the water bottle from the door handle, and flung the door open. Liz stood naked at the door, letting the cool air rush to replace the heat they'd generated in the sauna. From behind her, Ana stepped into the light, trailing her towel behind her.

Long distance

+++++ *Rita Speicher*

By noon it's too hot to walk barefoot on the beach stones. I wear my thongs to take the six steps from my towel to water's edge, carrying a blue float, nothing like the water, which today is green. I drift far from shore, but can still see the white house, the balcony with the clothesline Vera's now filling. Most of our clothes are white, though I have a coral sundress more popular than I imagined. When we bought my beach towel in the village we travel to once a week for food, I had a choice of green or orange. Vera chose green for me. I stood close to her holding the money. She asked how much and I thought I understood the merchant so I had the blue bills out of my pocket. This is one of her countries. Having never traveled, I compare it only to my own. "How far?" I asked before we left, meaning the distance between our village and the one with supplies. We had planned to start early that morning, but by the time we finished breakfast and made it to the car the sun was whitening toward noon, the blue sky perfected like an act of simple charity. We parked on a narrow side street and walked to the main thoroughfare, where Vera didn't notice men at the cafés follow her glide and profile. Vera's adventurous by inclination, not design, and if I had asked to stay, we might never have made it back to the States. The street was animated by outdoor stands crowded with fruit, fabric, shoes, unfamiliar herbs. We felt each native peach before handing bags of them to the owner, who approximated the weight. We bought fresh yogurt. I sat at an outdoor table, back-to-back with a priest in the full cloak of orthodoxy, watching Vera's hips cross the patio with my drink. After lunch we bought my towel and fresh butter cookies filled with apricot jam. Driving back, she nibbled at a vegetable pie, balancing it on her knee between bites, licking her fingers. We sang a few songs and fiddled with the radio. From time to time we looked at each other, surprised, absorbed. We had opened all the windows; dry breeze collected in back like a passenger. We yawned and held hands till the road curved again. Without translation I understood the political slogans painted on the mountains claiming victory for right wing and left wing. We passed one hitchhiker, smoldering in the afternoon heat, a wet bandana over her face like an outlaw. Once a red convertible passed, speeding in the other direction. Unloading the groceries, Vera asked, "Should we have picked her up?" and I, having forgotten, smiled at the endurance of her thought; preoccupied with a piece of music, hours might pass between a question and its answer. Vera would score her first libretto in the fall, a cabaret.

The beach is empty except for my towel. And my thongs at the shoreline, now nudged by the tide. I've been on the float longer than I expected, watching Vera hang laundry, then play a variety of instruments I can't hear from this distance — flute, dulcimer, sax — but recognize from the posture of her body. I paddle the float in a little circle, looking up: house, mountain, cloudless blue. Close to the peak everything is sanctified. When I rock, cool water trickles over the edge and I dam it between my thighs. Vera goes inside; first she waves, stands, turns. My thongs have drifted out, a few yards right, walking on water like an abandoned circus act. I slide in, tug the float with me. I haven't swum in water this clean since adolescence.

Heat radiates from the stones. The villagers don't come to the beach till six, after naps. I can actually see the heat waves, and the longer I watch the dizzier I become. A few times a young girl brought an old woman in traditional black and buried her under the stones except for her head, and once, by oversight, her big toe, which she looked at instead of the horizon. It's difficult to imagine grief on this coast; the common air suckled and amorous with slow, crazed heat. You dive into the day; it parts and swallows you. You become familiar with possibility as with an unrestrained woman. Even in the house, even napping on the cot, you're perched in the element.

Vera composes, with each instrument, distracted from sex. I've written postcards and perused science magazines. I've waited. Friends arrived. At dinner we tell funny stories — or those gouged with destiny and sex. Night after night on the balcony of the same mountain restaurant we look down to the sea and up to the constellations, eating our salad, smoking our cigaret as if everything were usual or permanent or belonged to a constant benefactor. When I don't sit next to Vera I sit across from her. When the table is round I blush into the expanse. To the villagers — Vera translates — we are the "five girls alone." In the house, I'm crowded from her.

I follow dizziness into the exhaustion of waking, heavy-limbed, on my towel, the contour of my smell like a drawing into which I unwittingly release the transmigratory and aloof sex code of telepathy. I want to swim and eat peaches. I want to lie down with Vera. I want to bake us on the stones with the slow drug of the sun. Vera's strolling down the beach. Straw hat, Walkman, black bikini. She's in no hurry, and smiles. When she lies next to me, we chat and harvest tiny shells. Vera salvages all the blushed ones from my pile, offering in exchange the white and purple she collected. One by one I take them, then lick the salt from the bowl of her palm. Each small act caresses the unspeakable with diversion — like a magician. We are talking about adolescent sex. I tell Vera a story she likes. I'm thirteen and it's a very hot night. I'm at my parents' summer bungalow colony. The owners open the pool for a midnight swim. The caretaker's son is blond and muscular. We swim together, short laps of the width at the deep end. When I rest against the edge, he finds my hands underwater. He is fifteen and treading without effort. He smiles his blue eyes. We swim in a little circle, holding hands. I'm laughing. He has a name like Buddy or Skipper. We're surrounded by adults and splashing peers. He takes my hand underwater and grazes his crotch with it. His eyes give nothing of accident or intent. I blush. Again my hand is near his crotch. He opens my palm and presses it to him. I look away, wave to friends with my free hand. He rubs my palm against him. I feel him pulse. Instantly I pull away, kick off, and swim to the other side of the pool. Someone connects the radio to the loudspeaker. The Platters are singing "My Prayer," and at the shallow end a bunch of boys mimic the lyrics and dunk one another. At the deep end other teenagers are hiding in the shadows under the diving boards, holding on to floats and forbidden anatomy while our parents' voices rise, compete, and finally coalesce to warn us not to stay in too long. Buddy or Skipper is swimming across to me, underwater. He surfaces slowly against my body, dragging his hands up the sides of my thighs, over my hips, up my torso, links them under my arms, his thumbs grazing the top of my one-piece, lifts me away from the edge of the pool, and drops me so I sink and surface, targeting his face with a fine spray from between my teeth. He dives under again. This time when he surfaces he drags his hands up the inside of my thighs. He rests one finger against my crotch. An immediate warmth collects and spreads to my thighs, into the cool water, like a dye; I look to see who notices. Our parents are beginning to leave or huddle around the card tables in the dark. The eighteen-year-olds are drifting through the gate to the other side of the bushes. My crowd is still in the water, howling, diving, hiding. His finger circles, then taps, then wanders to the elastic. He pulls on the band so water rushes in. His finger retreats and my hips thrust to follow. Two fingers on me now, pushing and circling. I come right away but he doesn't know and continues. He pulls at the elastic again and gets his whole hand in my suit. I wiggle against his palm. I'm wet different from the water. He slips one finger right up me and rubs my clit with his thumb. It feels like my heart needs to breathe. I try not to look in the direction of anybody, arching my neck to the stars, then come again. I do a back flip, stroke to the ladder, wave to him, and get out.

It's Vera's turn. She tells the one about her cousin who was not really her cousin. Then we wash a peach and remain at water's edge. Vera inhales her food. We walk the float into the water, hold on with our arms, and kick, sometimes tangling at the ankles. When we're out far enough to drift, Vera jumps on, unties the top of her bikini, and covers her face with it. I ride her around for a while, changing her view from mountain to village to water and sun. "Splash me a little," she mumbles through her bikini top. I drip water between her breasts. It snuggles down to the slight rise of her belly, mixing with sweat. Vera has toned, smooth abdominals, creamy olive skin. "More," she sighs. I hold on to the float with my elbows, cup water in my hands, and scoop it on to her chest. She massages the cool into her breasts and shoulders. "God, it's hot," she sighs. I pull down on the float, letting a little water over the edge. She wiggles it under her back and ass. I pull again. Willingly, she slides off, sinks under, her hair billowing on the water's surface like a sea flower come to life, while underwater her tongue grazes my collarbone. I wait for these moments like orbiting astronauts must wait for God. We float on our backs, arms stretched, fingers twined — then Vera's behind me, palms under my shoulder blades, offering me, a memento, to the sky. She glides me back to the float and when I pull my body out of the swoon of water I see her friends waving from the beach. They drop their towels like warnings next to ours, amble to the shore, wade to midcalf. Their eyes fix on us as if we're the lone attraction in this recluse beauty. Two are the color of instant cocoa; the other is praline. I help Vera onto the float.

We wobble and grab for each other. I clutch her elbow just as she catches the front of my bathing suit and we slide in opposite directions, Vera's torso over the side pulling my suit to my waist. Watched, we're both naked in their eyes now.

Some days Vera disappears through entire changes of light. Compelled, the rest of us enter an uneasy alliance. We brood. A motion at once solemn and hysterical collects us. Dance, it commands, and in the living room behind shades drawn against the broiling sun we turn into raucous athletic punks capable of a bitterness we mistake for irreverence. Talk, it insists, and lying on our bellies, we do as the stone balcony cools through dusk and the sentimental charms us with its small, inaccurate mysteries. All gone as soon as Vera returns, humming or occupied, and each of us, feigning indifference, shifts our unobstructed loyalty to the frustration we know as desire. I always want to kiss Vera; face it, I tell myself, delighted by the transparent. If seen from the outside, I would think us fictitious and funny. I would want to join us. I traveled here because Vera invited me, and if I were to follow the instinct connecting that bid to the future, witnessed literally like an image on a video screen, I had no choice but to arrive ready for the unconventional. It wasn't only a matter of faith. It was an opportunity to engrave the erotic with conscience.

Vera and I haul the float toward shore, Vera on her back lightly kicking. Deliberately, I'm the guide. I zigzag and waver. In the flat sea, I find corners to turn. I stall and lurch. If Vera said about face and head for the horizon, I'd obey. I'd marry her in this bathing suit. Naked I'd marry her, with or without brunch. Vera says nothing and I don't imagine she is waiting for me to say it. I surrender to the current. It lands us on the white lip of foam, ankle deep, where Vera's companions have waited. "Don't go," Vera whispers, so low I'm not certain I've heard it. I turn to her for confirmation. She's floating facedown. She lifts her head. "C'mon," she says. Now the five of us maneuver the float — comic, indolent — jerking us into deep water where finally we loll as if our comfort were always this casual. The sun bakes our heads. Mild current lifts and drops us. I hallucinate a foot between my knees, climbing like an infidel to the consecrated, till a sweep of toes across my crotch slams me against the real. I open my eyes. Vera's head is thrown back to the water and up to the sun, eyes closed, a smile, immodest and satisfied.

Before dinner I shower and lie out on the balcony. In the yard three white goats squat next to our white car. Scratchy tunes on the hi-fi from the house behind the bushes unravel into dusk. The sun strays in back of the mountain. I sing along with the best of the Everly Brothers — "All I Have to Do Is Dream," "Wake Up, Little Susie." Sometimes Vera is slow; she shifts her weight from one foot to the other and an afternoon goes by. Other times quick, like now, the brusque, transient thrill of lightning. She's wearing a peach halter, white skirt, and wants to borrow a sweater. We're the same height; once when measured back-to-back we remained attached long after the calculating hand withdrew, breathing together as though dancing. I'd like to ask Vera, was that your foot? was that permission swaddled in accident? is it time to kiss?

Later, the night-flowers' thick scent will loosen us like the wine we forget to buy, and straddling both it and Vera's fragrance I'll prepare the balcony with blankets. I sit across from Vera, patient as destiny, in whose cult I am stripped. I want to rouse the hidden from its fancy shaft. I want Vera to play me with her lips, like the sax inflated and gleaming under the black sky with its jackpot of stars. Spread on the blankets now, shoulder to shoulder. As the stars begin to dive in the flamboyant arcs of a meteor shower, I reach for Vera, twining her to me as if our clasped hands cradled a vow, and all my attention — vivid, mindful of a persuasion that donates the sexual — takes her to the spasm of surprised delight, the orgasm public and yielded, from which she cries mine.

Me and Charlie and her

Pam McArthur

✦✦✦✦

Well, I have to say it looked unlikely right from the start. Oh, sure, we had one thing in common, our love of horses, and I, at least, was hot for her like nobody's business. Why, that very first day when I looked up from currying Charlie and saw her walking into the barn, I just about dropped the currycomb, and I stood there staring so long that Charlie finally swung his old head around and nudged me to get going. There was just that something about her.

But I also knew for a fact that she belonged with the big bay horse who'd just moved into our stable, and he was in a different league entirely from my Charlie. This horse was a good seventeen hands high, and his coat was sleek as ice, his mane all trimmed and tidy, his hooves shiny from oiling.

That first day I watched — I couldn't help myself — as she got out a flat little nothing of a saddle, a sparkling white pad to go under it, and a bridle with too many reins on it for my liking. She didn't even curry the horse proper — just ran a soft brush over his back, and in two minutes flat she had him tacked up. She had to stretch herself up to reach the saddle onto his high withers. I was still smiling about the pretty picture that made when she led her horse out of the stable.

Then I turned back to Charlie and finished currying him, brushing out great handfuls of the winter hair he was still shedding. I got his beat-up old western saddle and a hackamore and finally we were ready; I led him out into the sparkling sunshine and swung up into the saddle. There's just nothing like sitting on the back of a good horse on a clear morning in April — life doesn't get any better, not to my way of thinking.

As I headed Charlie through the gate and across the upper pasture, I looked up at the outdoor riding ring and I just couldn't believe it. There she was on this gorgeous day when anybody else would've been riding through the fields and woods — there she was on her big bay horse riding circles in the dust. Big circles and little circles — I mean, what's the point? I knew right then and there that we didn't really have anything in common and I might as well put this woman out of my mind.

I did forget about her easily enough too, after Charlie and I had turned and jogged down the dirt trail to the woods beyond. We had a glorious long ride and I sure was feeling good when we finally ambled back into the stable yard — wore out but content to be alive in this world.

She was still there in the yard, just hanging around, when I rode in. She looked up at me — not very far up, 'cause nobody could ever accuse Charlie of being long-legged — and she smiled. As I slid off Charlie she gave us the once-over. Nice little horse, she said in this soft voice that near about melted me.

Well, as a general rule I'm not a sucker for anybody anymore, having been that road too many times already, but there is one thing I can't resist, and that's a pretty woman who appreciates my Charlie. So I grinned back at her, noticing how she wasn't really what most people would call pretty. Her face was warm and alive, though, and those brown eyes of hers, well, they weren't even really brown, they were more some kind of green with lots of brown flecks that made them seem ordinary brown until you looked up close. Which I suddenly realized I was doing, and maybe too close for somebody who hadn't even introduced herself yet, so I moved back a step and led Charlie away to rub him down.

After that first day, even though I kept telling myself to forget about her, I did sometimes look for her when I went out to ride. Maybe she was there and maybe she wasn't. When she was, we'd get to talking, and that was enough to make my fool heart hope that the very unlikely thing would turn out to be possible after all. I started in to thinking about her all the time, and pretty soon I was almost ready to ask her to come to my place on Saturday night for a get-together I was having with my oldest friends — you know, the kind who drop in on each other every couple of years to make sure we're all still alive. All the time I was getting ready for this get-together I got to admit I had this new woman in mind. I was just a sight in the kitchen as I whizzed around, fixing up all sorts of goodies.

Now, I know this surprises some, but I do a smart bit of cooking. Not just stuff like chili and lasagna, though I sure do like that too, but I can also bake the flakiest piecrust and even do some real fancy dishes when I want. My mama saw to that. Now she had in mind that cooking would help me catch a man — maybe she sensed even then that it was going to take some help — and probably my knowing her reasons was why at the age of sixteen I refused to set a useful foot in the kitchen. I didn't change my mind until years later when I fell head over heels in love and baked the fluffiest lemon meringue pie ever, I mean it was a pie you'd die for. That was in June, as I recall, and the prettiest June ever seen anywhere, but that was a long time ago.

After that I have always liked cooking for someone — the right someone — and I mooned around for a couple days thinking about all the delectables I could make for this woman, until I came to my senses and realized, of course, I couldn't ask her to this gathering: all my friends were women and 99 percent the same persuasion as me. And me not having a clue about which way the wind blew through her field, you know what I mean? I mean, I sure did hope she leaned the same way as me, but it wasn't likely. You can't trust your instincts with horsewomen, and that near about breaks my heart every time I think about it — all those good-looking outdoorsy women clearly more in love with their horses than with their husbands but not a one of them will admit it. They keep those men trailing along not good for anything but to pop up every now and then and remind me I'm not wanted. Me with as much love as the best of them, and so lonely some nights I go to sleep with the light on and my big stuffed Peter Rabbit wrapped in my arms, only don't you ever tell.

So the point is, I wasn't at all sure about this woman, had no reason to be more than the tiniest bit hopeful (and even that was stretching some), so I didn't ask her to my get-together. I had a fine old time anyway and was up till all hours, so the next morning I slept late and got up groaning. It was a dampish-feeling day anyway, more like it was heading back into winter instead of warming to summer like it was supposed to. So I took my time and washed up the dishes and all from the night before, and even had my laundry done and clean sheets on the bed before I finally sat down to a midday snack of last night's leftovers. I sat there at my old maple table, eating away and wondering if I was going to find the energy to go take old Charlie out. I do believe I would've just kept on sitting there wondering all afternoon if I hadn't peeked out the window and seen the sun coming out and all the damp trees sparkling in the light and the world looking pretty good after all.

So I found myself dressed and headed out to the stable, wondering if she was going to be there. Not likely, I told myself — it was pretty late in the day for her — so I strolled into the barn real casual, whistling through my teeth, my mind on nothing but Charlie and which trail we were going to ride. But as I turned down the aisle to Charlie's stall, there she was, just standing there. Talking to Charlie. And she says to me, real careless, I'm going out on the trails today; would you come along and show me around?

Would I? Well, my heart skipped around without asking permission, but I just said okay real smooth and easy, and got real busy with Charlie. Got him spiffed up extra good and wiped down his tack before putting it on him. He did look fine, my Charlie did, and I gave him a pat as we walked out of the barn. Don't get your hopes up, I whispered to him. This may be as tame as a walk in Central Park. Well, Charlie wouldn't know Central Park from Central America, so he ignored me and pricked his ears up and snorted and generally made a fuss as she rode her big bay up to us.

She just smiled at me and kept her horse alongside Charlie as we headed toward the woods. That day, that cold and dampish day, was turning out to be real pretty after all. The sun kept ducking out from behind those don't-mean-no-harm clouds, and the woods were all speckled with sunlight and baby green leaves. We walked up a narrow bit of trail and came to this old logging road that Charlie and I love, and we put our horses into an easy gallop and rocked along side by side. I was so happy, I could've burst out singing, except I'm none too famous for my voice and I don't generally try it out on anyone else — certainly not someone I might, if there's any point to it, be trying to impress.

Well, I was busy just thinking about her, when all of a sudden I saw we were at this bend in the road. Just around the bend I knew there was a big old oak tree down across the trail, and I do mean big. The top of that log was four feet high if it was anything, and solid tree right down to the ground. So, remembering this, I pulled Charlie up and called to her to do the same. But she cantered on around the bend and I worried some as I followed her. I came around the corner just in time to watch her canter steadily at that damn log, and then rise lightly out of the saddle as the two of them sailed right over. Cleared it like it was nothing and kept right on down the road.

And even from the back, and as far away as I was, it did look like she was laughing with the fun of it.

Well, Charlie and I jogged around the end of that fallen tree — its roots waving every which way in the air like they were still trying to figure out where the ground had got to — and then we lit out at a dead run to catch that bay horse. That afternoon surely was a revelation to me. She never over-stretched her horse, but she did ride him hard both uphill and down, and that bay took everything in stride and always with one ear perked forward like he was saying that was fun — what's next?

So it wasn't a Central Park sort of ride at all, and I was liking the looks of this woman a whole lot. In fact, the more we chased after her the better she looked. It seemed like no time at all to me before the afternoon was gone and we were on the homeward stretch. We walked our hard-worked horses the last bit so they were cooled down and breathing normally when we walked into the stable yard. Which is more than I could say for myself — I wasn't neither cooled down nor breathing normal as I watched her leap off her horse and turn to me, her face shining, those brown-green eyes looking right at me. Thanks was all she said, though. And you're welcome is all I said, as I led Charlie into the barn and fussed over him a bit more than usual, not looking around to see what she might be up to. I wasn't sure it was safe to watch her too much, not till I'd got my feelings back under control. But while I was still sweet-talking Charlie she come along and leaned herself over his stall door. She smiled at me and damned if I didn't feel myself grinning back at her like a fool.

A good ride like that sure wakes up my appetite, she said in that honey voice of hers. I couldn't exactly come out and tell her what appetites of mine were waking up just from looking at her, but I did say we could get a bit to eat at my place if she felt like it. I could hardly keep my voice steady, just offering that much, but she must not have noticed, 'cause she agreed as calm as you please.

When we got to my place she strolled right in as if she'd been there a dozen times before. She stood there looking around and smiling at all my things like they were exactly how she knew they'd be, and me, I just stood there watching her till all of a sudden I remembered how grubby I was from our ride. I said to her, I'd better get cleaned up — you just make yourself right at home. She grinned and said, you bet I'll do that. So I left her standing there and I ran into the bathroom. I shucked out of my clothes in no time flat and jumped into the shower, all the time thinking of her actually there in my living room. Well, I had just gotten a good soapy lather worked all over me and started the most improbable fantasy in my mind when I heard the shower curtain squeak open and there she stood. Stark raving naked. I was so shocked I near about peed my pants except, of course, I wasn't wearing any. She just said real cool, I figured we could save water, and in she stepped. Well, I swear the temperature in there jumped about a hundred degrees, but I was determined to play just as cool as her.

I did peek at her a little though. I couldn't help myself. Up close and personal like that I could see that her body was beginning to settle, getting comfortable the way a grown woman's will. And I loved her for that. Then I got afraid I was staring more than was proper, so I turned my back on her — oh, that was hard! — and ducked my head under the water. I was shaking the water out of my eyes when I felt her move close to me and her hands slipped around me and stroked my front, collarbone to breast to down as far as she could reach, then back up to do it again. I never felt anything like her hands before in all my life. Me all slicked up with soap like that, and that steamy water streaming down my front side, and her softness pressing me behind; I knew for a fact that I had died and gone to heaven.

I felt her nuzzle her face into the back of my neck as her hands slid all over me. Soon I was shaking so bad I didn't think I could stand up anymore and I turned and looked straight into her green eyes and I said, what do you want to do? Dumb question probably, but I still couldn't believe what was happening and I had to be sure I wasn't about to make a big mistake.

This woman, she waited a heartbeat, then said, whatever you want — and then some.

Well, hearing her say that, I turned the water off and I took her to my bed. Both of us were still dripping wet but not minding one bit. I laid her down real gentle, and I kissed and nibbled my way from her face down her long slender throat to the ridge and hollow of her collarbone. My hands crept down to her breasts and held them a minute as if they were the biggest miracle ever, then I started stroking them and rubbing at her nipples. Real soft at first, but when she started to moan and gripped my back hard and dug her nails in, I just cut loose and rubbed and pulled and teased and felt her nipples grow hard under my hands. I leaned down and sucked her into my mouth, wrapping my tongue around the nipple and pulling it through my teeth while she went wild, groaning and bucking and pulling me close to her. Oh, she was something! I couldn't get enough of her. I touched her all over, everywhere, and she just kept on rocking and shaking and loving every bit of it. I slid myself down to her thighs, and I hesitated to open them, but she spread them for me herself, crying oh yes!

With a groan I lay down between her legs and took her full wet flesh into my mouth. I sucked and bit and held on like a woman drowning while she rocked under me. She thrust herself hard against my mouth until at last she cried out with such pleasure I near about died.

And then she turned to me and started running her hands all over me, coming back always to my breasts, stroking and tugging and teasing till I was shivering deep down inside. She looked at me with such fire in those green eyes that when her searching hand stroked its way down my belly and over my hips, well, I spread my legs shamelessly wide for her. I wanted her touch there like I've never before wanted anything. And when she did touch me, spreading my wet all around and rubbing it over and over that little nub of flesh, I started rocking that bed hard and fast and crying out. It was like sparklers bursting all over me. I thought I couldn't take any more, not and live to tell the tale, but then she gave me still more and I *did* take it all. And lived. And she kissed me again, her eyes shiny with tears, and she rocked me till we both fell asleep all tangled up in each other.

So now here I lie, having waked myself up before even the first chirp of dawn, and I'm thinking this all through, how it happened. And I still got to say it looked unlikely right from the start, but here I look down and I see her sleeping angel's face wrapped up in my arms, and I just lie here smiling as I wait for the breaking light of day.

Sea witch

◆◆◆◆ *Patricia Roth Schwartz*

Cara's first impression of the Seawitch Inn, so highly recommended by her co-workers Annie and Rachel, was how full it seemed to be of women! The impression remained even when she obeyed the note that said, "Out shell hunting! Let yourself in. You're in the Lavender Room, top of the house," and stepped through the wide, carved-oak double doors paneled in stained glass, into the sun-flooded parlor, and found herself alone. Women's faces, bodies, the fragrance of women, a women's sensibility, infused the atmosphere...

Sculptures of goddesses, fecund, powerful, and holy, stood on almost every surface; paintings of women — the solitary, somber faces of old women, sorceresses, or the young, embracing bodies of joyful women friends — leapt from embossed frames on almost every wall. The colors of the walls, rugs, furniture throws, curtains, cushions were women's colors — sand, shell, pearl, earth. The heady musk of incense recently burned brought to Cara's nostrils a sense of longing so intense she had to sink to the soft couch piled with embroidered cushions and pillows and catch her breath.

Just the long journey from Boston, she told herself. *Buses are so tiring. What I need is a cup of tea.* She urged herself up and over to the compact yet well-appointed kitchen that inhabited the lower end of the long room, separated from the living area by a divider of open, beautifully varnished pine shelves on which more goddesses, dainty ones in dancing poses, resided, along with glass jars of herbs, pottery mugs, and fat candles of many sizes and colors. Cara helped herself to a mug and a handful of herbs from a jar marked "Sweet Repose." She steeped and strained them, then wandered out to the typically New England–seacoast porch, long, narrow, lined with stiff-backed, rush-seated rockers that faced the sea. She sat as she suspected generations of women had sat, their eyes as wide and deep as the ocean that filled all of the middle distance and swallowed the horizon. Like them, she was looking and watching and waiting — would what she hoped for ever have a name? Would it, like a long-lost ship, or the tide, ever come in?

This getaway week was to be a gift to herself from herself. Annie and Rachel and others of her friends had urged it. The long hours at the clinic caring for those who never got better, facing the tragedies not so much of disease and inevitable death but of agencies without funds, callous social services, families who turned their backs, friends who were always coming in "tomorrow," lovers who had already died or fled in terror, had taken its toll.

"You need to pay attention to just *you*," Annie had said. She and her lover, Rachel, adored the Seawitch Inn, run by two women friends of theirs, Zoe, a weaver, and Jane, an artist, who earned a living taking in paying guests (women only) six months of the year and doing their artwork full-time on the modest proceeds.

"But I'll be out of place." Cara had never had a problem with the lifestyle of her friends. The clinic itself, dealing with what it did, of course, had many gay clientele and staff; she herself was the different one there. Yet Cara was sensitive, as she had been all her life, about not being quite like everybody else; about standing as she could remember doing on the playground, in a new school, with no friends yet, as teams were chosen; about being the "odd girl out."

"No — no — it's a place for *women,*" her friends assured her. "Don't worry — no one will make a pass at you!"

"Maybe they should!" Cara returned with a wicked grin. She'd definitely learned to play and tease — something unheard of in her life before — since meeting these two and the others at the clinic. A certain bizarre sense of humor seemed to help them all to cope. Besides, as the only straight woman among lesbians, she was bound to get razzed about when she was coming out.

"Now, Cara, you know it's a myth that lesbians seduce straight women — at least those who don't want to be seduced!" Rachel had gone on, grinning back at her.

Now, as Cara watched the gulls wheel and dive, as small boats chugged or glided over the picture-postcard harbor, soft in the singing daylight, awash with all the variations of blue and mauve and dove gray a painter's palette could have contained, Cara wondered, where was her heart?

This place felt as though it held her in the palm of its hand. She knew she wasn't minding being alone — or without Rob. The demise of that relationship, the first and only one of some length she had ever really had, had left her bruised of soul and weary but not devastated. As it was, his choice to devote most of his energies to political activism, the Central American struggle, and a local coalition for the homeless had left her a grass widow of sorts for many months before their breakup.

Their few sessions of couples counseling had confirmed the mismatch. The counselor had constantly pointed out Cara's need for nurturing (the coldness of her parents, her family's many moves, the draining work she did) and Rob's need not to feel that he, as the son of a particularly demanding alcoholic mother, must sacrifice his goals to take care of someone else. It was all just too sad, and a perfect article for a New Age therapy journal. Rob and Cara, now separated, met occasionally for cups of espresso and stilted conversation at the Che

Guevara Bookstore and Café, and went on with their own lives.

I'm fine, Cara told herself, draining the last of the surprisingly invigorating tea. She bundled into a thick Irish sweater, a souvenir of a college student tour of her grandmother's land of birth, and stalked off down the sloping lane to the rocky beach to watch the sun finally sink, glorious, beneath the earth's curve.

She slept that night — window flung open to the tangy sea air (which made her feel as the incense had earlier) — to the comforting soft sounds of the foghorns in the vast and soothing darkness.

At breakfast, her hostesses and their four cats all pounced on her with a friendly welcome. "There won't be any other guests till the weekend," they told her. "We're off to exhibit our wares at a crafts fair in Bar Harbor. The place is literally all yours till Friday. Just put food out for the beasts and shut the windows if we get a squall. You don't need to lock the door, and the answering machine will take all calls. No one will bother you," Jane said, gathering her light, fringed shawl about her and hoisting her bulging straw tote bags full of weavings to load up the van.

"Except maybe the resident ghost," Zoe winked playfully, reminding Cara of Annie. *I must have "tease me" written all over my face,* she thought. Zoe hefted a parcel of canvases to her hip and grabbed the picnic basket handle. "I'm sure one little ghost won't bother you."

"Of course not," Cara played along. "I assume it's a friendly one." She'd been dreaming over her cooling cup of tea about a long hike up to the wild blueberry field they'd told her about, but this story piqued her interest. Her grandmother, Alana, from Galway, had had many tales of "things that go bump in the night." Cara didn't know whether to be scared or intrigued — or just to take a joke for what it was.

"Yes, it's a friendly ghost — Miss Bethany Hopkins. You can read all about her in that little brochure from the Chamber of Commerce. Stone Harbor will capitalize on anything vaguely historical to rake in the tourists. Yes — even if it's about a woman — and a witch at that! We named the inn after her — even though we've never heard her. The two old ladies who lived here at the turn of the century claimed they heard her singing every night, and the legend was born."

"Come on, you silly romantic," Zoe urged her partner, "enough of old wives' tales. We'll be late. Cara can hold her own here, I'm sure."

And suddenly Cara was alone. Idly, she picked up the brochure and took it, with a fresh cup of tea, to the porch. All she learned from reading was that Captain Josiah and Sarah Hopkins had owned the house and that their only daughter, Bethany, had died young, allegedly of a broken heart over a lover lost at sea. Years ago it was claimed that she could be heard singing a lament for him. In a few minutes, though, Cara was bored; she felt again the call of the blueberries. Spooky stories were either for the tourists or those long-gone days when she'd sat at Grandmother Alana's knee, holding her skein of wool as the old woman spun yarns as well as yarn.

Later that afternoon, after her hike, Cara picked through the two quarts of blueberries she'd gathered and ate a heaping serving over vanilla yogurt. She followed her snack with a blissful nap, then another walk, and a pleasant supper at the nearby fish 'n' chips shop, where the locals' talk was full of commonplace town gossip, nothing eerie or otherworldly. When she returned to the inn, Cara sank into her white-painted iron bedstead under a rainbow-hued patchwork quilt, ready to relax with one of the numerous, tempting paperbacks that overflowed the end tables and shelves of every corner of the inn. The books were of history, biography, poetry, myth, art — all by and about women. Cara chose one and settled in. Above her, stars sprinkled the velvet patch of sky the small skylight revealed. For the first time she could remember since those afternoons with Grandmother Alana, she felt blessed.

Sleep must have claimed her without her knowing it. When she awoke, the bedside lamp still glowed but the constellations framed by the skylight were different. The book had slithered to the floor. Two of the cats slumbered heavily across her shins. The covers were disarrayed.

What was I reading? A vivid tale of Bethany Hopkins, the tragic young maid of Stone Harbor, was singing in her head. Yet her book had been about women artists in Paris of the 1920s. *I must have dreamt it.* Cara snapped off the light and started to arrange herself for sleep. The usually cool temperature of the seacoast had mysteriously shifted. The room felt oppressively hot and stuffy.

I don't need this. Cara stood up and stripped off her fine, white, lace-edged lawn gown, one she'd found on sale in a shop of Victoriana. Its virginal design had comforted her after her breakup with Rob. *I'm just not very sexy,* she told herself. Coupling with Rob, although he'd been gentle enough and concerned for her pleasure, had seemed to do little for her. "All that effort for such a small reward," she'd quipped and consigned herself to celibacy and good works. Now her body's reflection caught her glance suddenly in the full-length, oval, wood-framed mirror that rested on a stand in the corner of the room. *There must be moonlight,* her thoughts registered. She could see herself clearly — yet as if in a dream. For an instant, the figure of the woman — with small yet rounded breasts, nipples like the bursting buds of the salt-spray roses she'd seen on her walk, firm stomach, and flanks creamy and smooth in the unexpected light, converging to a center where dusky hair fanned out in a V; the hair of her head loose and tousled, not in its everyday pulled-back style; her shoulders sloping and soft-looking — seemed to be not her, but another. It was as though a woman not herself yet very like her shared the room. She could still smell the musky incense from downstairs. A cloud must have moved over the moon. The reflection dimmed. Cara felt suddenly chilled. Her nipples grew tight and hard; her thighs prickled with goose bumps. She jumped back under the covers and pulled the quilt over her. Snuggling down, nonplussed by her uncharacteristic behavior (she couldn't recall ever having really looked at herself nude), she recalled vividly the story she must have dreamt.

Bethany had been speaking: "Yes, they all think it was a young man, my lover, who drowned. But, no, it was my beloved Rebecca, a girl who desired the lilt and swell of the sea as much as she did the pungent sea-taste of my loins, the green of my eyes, and the fire of my kisses. She set sail for the Horn dressed as a cabin boy. 'Just one adventure, I promise,' she swore to me on the breakwater the night before she stowed away. 'Then I'll be back to you, my love. We'll settle down as spinster schoolmarms with our seaside gardens full of marigolds and lupine and our cats, and no one will know that late after the church tower chimes, I'll sneak in darkness into your chamber and sleep naked, wrapped around your long legs, my head on your tender breast.' And then she opened my bodice to the night and suckled my nipples, one after the other, and slid her hand down into the layers of my petticoats and pantaloons to find that secret bud only she had taught me how to awaken, and coaxed it with her finger into a burst of joy. This was all I would have to remember of her — since she went down in a great storm off the tip of Africa with all the crew and never came home again. I took our secret to the grave, but find not rest there. It is women I seek — and one woman in particular, the one who will give me my heart's ease."

"What a bizarre tale!" Cara mused, bothered a bit by the frank eroticism. She felt herself on the edge of sleep, wanting to forget the night's events. *I must remember to tell Annie and Rachel,* was her last thought before she dropped into a deep well of slumber.

The next morning she was startled to awaken nude, the covers tossed back, her thighs open; between them she was wet. Lowering her fingers to the moisture, then raising them to her lips, she tasted the tang of the sea. Her nipples felt sore.

Even though the sun was warm they were hard and tight. Quickly she roused herself and showered and dressed, and set off, a lunch in her pack, for another hike, intentionally pushing herself so that she'd sleep long and hard — and dreamlessly — that night.

Yet once again, at a late hour, she was awake — pulled just from the edge of slumber by the plaintive cadence of a sea chanty, not the rollicking kind, but one that spoke of the cold deep and lovers lost. *Must be the café down the road,* she told herself, rolling over and pulling up the quilt. She'd worn her nightgown that night — its high lace collar tickled her throat. *Sometimes the local kids get rowdy down there.* She consigned herself to sleep again.

Yet there came a gentle touch to her shoulder — and as if in a trance she turned as though she were facing someone with the length of her body, letting the covers slip down. Any fear she might have had momentarily ebbed away. She floated now on the crest of a wave of peace and calm, an utterly safe place. She felt gentle fingers at her throat, one by one undoing the pearl buttons, accompanied by a silken brushing at her temples, across her cheeks, as if the long tresses of a woman were caressing her. She could smell a clean-hair smell, of sunshine and chamomile shampoo, under a scent of lavender and rose water. Gentle kisses, too, began to rain on her forehead and cheeks, as the gown seemed to slip away — bit by bit — from her shoulders.

The kisses became bolder — moved closer to her mouth. Cara was amazed that she was not at all frightened, only amazingly aroused, open and aflame as never before. She found herself opening her mouth, opening as if to take in all the passion and desire she'd been without for so long. Another mouth, unseen, met hers, lips sensuous yet seeking, and a sprightly tongue began to dance a teasing dance with hers as she felt hands travel the skin of her shoulders, arms, flanks ... The tongue became more insistent, found its way deeper; her mouth opened wider, seemed to ask as much of the other as was given; the hands, which were firm, warm, and deft, cupped her buttocks now, gently squeezing, urging her thighs apart. She was on her back. The unseen lover was above her. She could smell the essence of love, a woman's love, which pulled her into those same feelings of longing she'd had before but now could identify. This time there was no sorrow — as though she knew at last her longing was at an end.

The silken hair moved all over her body, her stomach, her thighs, her breasts. The kisses found their way there, too. The tongue caressed each nipple — one after the other — until they were tingly and almost sore. Those eager lips began to travel downward all over her stomach and loins, relentlessly closing in on that long-protected center, her legs opening wide to the night and the starlight and the far distant sound of the sea. First, a lapping tongue, and then strong fingers, entered her — deep, deep, powerfully moving into her, an exquisite pleasure — yet with an intensity she almost couldn't bear. Only when she willed herself to open just that much further did the pleasure overtake her wholly, the presence of another inside of her belonging as never before. The tongue had not ceased its lapping, either. Cara surrendered absolutely to what she had never before had — as that swell and break of the wave she had been riding brought tears to her eyes. Strong, warm arms enfolded her. Another cheek was laid against hers, the silken hair wrapped around her face and neck.

The sleep she slept then was the deepest she had known. All through the night she was not alone, legs wrapped around her legs, a head at her breast. In the morning, she awoke nude, in wildly disarrayed, pungent sheets, to full daylight flooding the room. The cats, hungry, were in the hall, keeping a distance as if they were wary of entering the room. Downstairs was noise and bustle. "Cara, we're back — get up, lazybones! Come out with us. We're borrowing a boat! We'll go clamming up at the point." It was Zoe and Jane. They'd sold all their wares the first day of the fair and had decided to come home for a day of play. Cara showered quickly, washing off all traces of what she was still telling herself was a dream. As she washed, her fingers and tongue began to tingle. They seemed to hold memories of having traveled the same terrain on a lover's body as the lover's had on hers.

The next day passed quickly. Unexpected guests showed up at the inn, sparking a blur of activity that culminated in a lobster bake out back. The following night, the new women trooped in late and giggled in their room till three a.m. Cara read and finally slept fitfully near dawn, till the cats bothered her for breakfast. She was glad now to be leaving, the spell the place had first cast on her having been broken, and she packed quickly, said perfunctory goodbyes to Zoe and Jane, who looked bewildered and a little hurt.

"We hope you had fun. Sorry about the new arrivals. We spoke to them about the noise."

"Sure. That's okay. I had a nice time."

"The ghost didn't get you?" Jane tried for a laugh.

"I don't believe in ghosts," Cara countered stiffly, already thinking of her appointment calendar at work and all she must do.

"Too bad. We've been hoping someone would spot her and tell us if that portrait over the fireplace really is of Bethany. It's supposed to be, you know. We found it at a local antique shop and got it for a song because the frame had been damaged. The new frame isn't bad, though, don't you think?"

The face was elfin, the locks silky, the eyes full of green fire, yet suffused with a deep tenderness touched with a grief kept deeply buried. The shoulders above the low-cut gown were creamy and soft. As Cara stared, entranced, the tip of a tongue appeared to dance behind the sensuous lips, which were just a bit open.

Shaking herself, Cara gathered her small bag and her purse and raced to the wharf for the bus that boarded down at the end of the dock. She bought a magazine at the dockside convenience store, settled into her seat, and took out a ripe peach. Zoe and Jane had pressed on her a bag lunch with a sandwich and some fruit. Cara had just bitten into the peach, felt her teeth sink beneath the delicate skin, tasted on her tongue the tart-sweet juice, when a woman boarded. She was about Cara's age, fit and tanned, with long, shiny hair that was casually pulled up and tucked under a fisherman's cap. Her faded blue chambray shorts and halter top showed off her lovely thighs, her delicious breasts. Her eyes were as green as the sea.

"Mind if I sit here?" The bus was empty except for the two of them.

"N-no, of course not—" Cara gestured the woman to the empty seat next to her, her heart beginning to pound.

"It's a long ride to Boston," the woman said in a musical voice. "Maybe we could get to know each other. I'm Beth."

"How did you know where I was going?" Cara asked.

The woman did not answer, just looked over at her with the face of the portrait in the Seawitch Inn and smiled.

Spelunking

++++ *Wendy Caster*

It was 1977, I had just come out, and I wanted desperately to get laid. At twenty-three years old, I was the last virgin on earth. But I didn't know any lesbians.

I worked in a print shop as the "customer service rep," which meant I was the one you yelled at when someone in the back fucked up. My co-workers were all male. They were okay, but I was never attracted to men who keep pictures of airbrushed women with gigantic breasts on the wall. I was never attracted to any men. They had hair on their chests. They smelled funny. And they didn't have breasts. They didn't have vaginas.

You see, I wanted to go spelunking.

I had discovered spelunking at the library when I stopped in to see what they had about lesbians. I found a book called *Lesbian/Woman,* but I was frightened to be seen reading it, so I wrapped it in a *Life* magazine. Then I turned to the section on "what women do together," and before I realized it, my hips were gently rocking back and forth on the small wooden library chair. I stopped my movement and looked around, but no one had noticed.

I closed the book, arranged the *Life* magazine over it, and tried to think of other things. It was embarrassing to feel hot in a library. But all I could think of were vaginas. The idea of putting my finger or tongue — tongue! — inside another woman sent sheets of lightning through my insides. The idea of a woman inside me was equally thrilling. But I was in a public place. This was not the time to think of vaginas. No vaginas, no vaginas, don't think of vaginas! For a second I made my brain blank. Then I saw a long pink tunnel. Then a cave. It was time for a walk.

I roamed through the stacks. The musty odor of old paper was enormously erotic. To distract myself, I grabbed the nearest book. It was called *Spelunking*. The subtitle was *The Art of Exploring Caves*. Yes, yes, yes! I wanted to explore caves! I checked the book out and went home.

The next day, they hired a woman to run the press at work. This was considered a male job, but no man would accept the lousy salary we paid.

The woman's name was Terry, and she was tall, with short curly brown hair, almost iridescent green eyes, and a perfectly round face. She wore a blue checked work shirt, 501 jeans, and beat-up cowboy boots. The second I looked at her, I was fantasizing about spelunking again — and praying that she was a lesbian. And single. And attracted to me.

That afternoon, while the guys were at lunch, Terry did a wonderful thing. She went around the shop and removed all of their pinups, leaving the dirty green walls checked with light green rectangles. She treated the pictures gently, rolling them into one of the tubes we used for delivering posters and leaning the tube against the men's room door. Then she put a small picture of Virginia Woolf on the wall next to the press.

I was in love.

I fidgeted, waiting for the guys to return. I pictured Terry standing her ground, strong and proud, until they admitted they were sexist pigs and promised to change their ways.

Reality was less romantic. The guys came back in a flurry of "wha' the fuck" and "who the hell." It was obvious the culprit was Terry, so Joe, the boss, went right up to her.

"Did you take down our pictures?"

"Yes." Terry looked Joe so strongly in the eyes that he looked down at his shoes. Then he looked up again and said, "Why?"

"I refuse to work in a sexist workplace."

This was greeted with another chorus of "wha' the fuck." Joe said, "They're just pictures. They don't do any harm."

Terry replied, "They support the mistreatment of women."

The men's curses grew louder.

Joe said, without much conviction, "You'll have to put up with them or leave." He was probably praying she would stay; with no one to run the press, he would have to work fourteen-hour days.

"Then I'm gone." She turned to go.

"Wait!" I was surprised to hear myself speak. "Joe, she's right. Those pictures are awful. If she goes, I go."

Joe's mouth fell open. He turned to the men behind him. "Hey, fellas, what do you say we give the girls a little slack here?"

The chorus grunted their refusals.

Joe turned back to Terry and me. "Do you have to leave?"

"Yes." We said the syllable together.

Joe slunk to his office. Terry took her picture of Virginia Woolf and her denim jacket. I grabbed my windbreaker. As we were leaving, one of the men said, "Hey, Julie, why are you quitting with that dyke?"

"'Cause I'm a dyke too."

I felt light suddenly, but powerful at the same time. My chest felt like it was filled with helium, and I floated out of the shop. Outside, Terry grinned and invited me to her apartment for chamomile tea.

Her apartment was wonderful. Its two rooms were sunny and large, with walnut molding around the windows and doors. Pictures of women filled every inch of wall space. Amelia Earhart. Gertrude Stein. Greta Garbo. Terry had to tell me who some of them were. Jeanette Rankin, the first woman elected to Congress. Mother Jones. Emma Goldman. I had a few years of college under my belt, but I had a lot to learn.

The apartment didn't have much furniture. The kitchen had a table and two chairs, and the other room had a desk, a chair, a bookcase crammed with books, and a mattress on the floor, covered with a brown-and-lavender Mexican blanket. As Terry prepared the tea, I sat at the kitchen table and we discussed the asshole men at work.

"I knew it probably wouldn't work out," Terry said. "I almost never work with men. But I had a couple of weeks before I left town, and I thought I'd make some extra money."

Left town!

Terry was moving to the Northwest to live in a women's commune. "I'm sure you know all about lesbian separatist politics," she said.

"No," I told her. "I don't know anything. I just came out, and I don't know any lesbians."

She turned to me with two cups of tea and a big smile. "Well, now you do."

I took my cup of tea and put it on the kitchen table, but she motioned me into the other room. "It's lighter in there," she explained. "And you can see this great tree out the window." She went to the mattress and sat on it, her back against the wall. She patted the spot next to her for me to sit on.

I wanted to be near Terry, but I was scared, so I feigned great interest in a glass donkey on her bookcase. Terry watched me with an amused grin, then said, "Come on, sit down." She patted the mattress again.

As I sat, my jeans slithered between my legs, and I realized I was wet just from being alone with a woman, this woman, this *lesbian*. Would I finally get to go spelunking?

Did I actually know how?

As we sipped our tea, she told me about separatist politics and the importance of being woman-identified. She told me that some lesbians were heterosexually identified, particularly the butch/femme crowd, but they weren't real lesbians. They hadn't caught up with the present.

As we talked, we watched the leaves sway on the giant tree outside the window, which tinted the room a glowing green. It was hard to concentrate on anything but Terry's shoulder next to mine.

Terry reached over and put our empty cups on the floor. Then she turned to me and ran her finger down my cheek, then across my lips. All the energy in my body flew to my face to be near her touch, and I blushed. She smiled, then kissed me. Her kiss sent intensified energy back into my body. My veins were tubes of red-flashing neon. She pulled me down onto the mattress and held me tight while gently stroking my tongue with hers.

There was a rush in my body as all my molecules clambered to be right next to Terry. My breasts were glowing. My toes were clenching and unclenching. And my brain was murmuring, "Finally, finally" — and also, "Oh, God, I hope I don't make a fool of myself."

Terry pulled slightly away from me and undid the buttons of my work shirt while kissing my neck. I wanted to undress her too, but buttons seemed impossible to deal with while my body went up and down and all around on its carousel. Instead, I stroked Terry's back, then reached under her shirt. I was startled by the smooth warmth of her skin. I had never touched anything so sweet, so beautiful, so ... touchable. I suddenly understood that matter and energy really were the same.

Terry rolled me onto my back. She leaned over me and kissed my clavicles, my breastbone, and then my breasts. I would have swooned, but I didn't want to miss anything.

Terry took my nipple into her mouth and the world stopped. There was nothing but my nipple and her mouth. The universe was focused on the tiny space where her tongue moved back and forth. I realized I was digging my fingers into her back and I stopped, scared I had hurt her — though she didn't seem to mind. She was crooning a sex song deep in her throat.

After a while, she sat up, grinned at me, and said, "We have altogether too much clothing on here." She shucked her shirt and jeans, then her underwear. She was stunning. Her shoulders were big and broad. Her clavicles were deep and elegantly defined. Her breasts were tiny round pyramids with large brown tips. Her pubic hair wandered down a thin line from her belly button to a lush triangle of growth hiding the cave where I might soon be spelunking. I moaned, then blushed again. I had never made a noise like that before in my life.

Terry laughed. "Aren't you going to take off your clothes?"

I was so lost in her body that I had forgotten mine. My shirt was easy to remove, since Terry had already unbuttoned it, but I had trouble with my jeans. I couldn't remember how a zipper worked. I felt like a jerk — wasn't sex supposed to be smooth and graceful? — but Terry helped me get my pants off. My underpants made a loud slurp as she removed them from between my legs. I blushed yet again, embarrassed to be so extravagantly wet, but Terry seemed pleased. She seemed pleased about everything.

Terry lay down on the mattress, and I stretched next to her on my side. Slowly, carefully, I reached out and touched her breasts. My breasts were large and pendulous, but hers were petite and firm, and her nipples hardened to tickle the insides of my palms. My hands had never been so happy.

Terry moved my hands from her breasts, then pulled me on top of her. When I felt the full sensation of her skin against mine, I yelped. She giggled, then whispered in my ear, "I'm so glad I'm your first." Her breath made the fuzzy hair along my back quiver. We held each other tightly, breasts to breasts, belly to belly, thighs to thighs. So this was why the world was so obsessed with sex! I was surprised anyone ever got out of bed.

Terry started rocking slowly, so I rocked with her. Then she moved one of her legs so that her thigh was against my clit, and I moved one of my legs in the same way. We rocked together faster, then faster still, moaning and panting. Terry's moans changed to groans as we rocked and bucked. Then she roared, and I realized she was coming. Wow! I didn't know you could come like that! I felt her orgasm in my breasts and stomach and insides, and tears came to my eyes. Terry relaxed under me, then looked at me with a lopsided grin. "You're sure a sexy beginner," she said. I felt like I had won the Nobel Prize in Human Relations.

We held each other for a while, then Terry said, "Now it's your turn." She rolled me over onto my back, then started stroking me all over my body. I was like a kitten, raising each body part to her touch, purring, and wanting more. She kissed my belly and my hips, then my pubic hair. My cave swelled into a cavern, preparing a welcome for Terry.

Terry arranged herself between my thighs and resumed kissing me. She opened me with her tongue and drew circles around my clit. The whole mess of my twenty-three years of life now made sense; it was all so I could get to this moment. Energy spasmed throughout my body and my head rolled back and forth. A storm cloud was gathering in my loins, and lightning was going to strike. And my cave yelled, "Come inside me, please, please." Terry licked me and licked me. The storm cloud grew. My cave yelled, "Fuck me, please!" Terry didn't hear. Soon I didn't care about anything but her tongue and my clit. Soon after that, I came, a glorious, muscular, liquid come.

We made love two more times that evening, and it was incredible. But Terry never explored my cave, and when I tried spelunking her, she gently but firmly pulled my hand away.

Later, she explained why. "You see, Julie, penetration is male-identified, so lesbians don't do it."

"All lesbians?" I asked.

"All real lesbians," she answered and handed me some books about woman-identified sex.

I didn't dare tell Terry how very much I craved spelunking, and for the next two weeks we had nonstop sex — her way. It was wonderful, but I still wanted ... more.

Terry moved to the Northwest, and I went job hunting. And lover hunting. After my adventure with Terry, I felt braver about going to lesbian rap groups. I read the books she gave me, and I learned a lot about lesbian behavior. *Robert's Rules of Order* seemed simpler, but I adjusted. After all, these women had carefully thought things through. Who was I to second-guess them?

I had occasional affairs but still no spelunking. When I masturbated, I would fuck myself furiously, but then I would feel guilty. I didn't want to be male-identified. I wanted to be a real lesbian.

A couple of months after I met Terry, I discovered the spelunking book, long overdue at the library, in the back of my car. I leafed through it and sighed, remembering when I believed that once I found women, my cave would get all the exploration it desired. Then I went to the library to return the book.

As I waited to find out how much I owed, a woman got in line in back of me. She was in her forties and large and round. She wore a long skirt, an Indian print blouse, and a fedora. She smiled at me, and I was pretty sure we were both deciding the other was a lesbian. I'm not sure how I knew about her; she didn't dress the right way or anything. Maybe she didn't know the rules. Which meant, maybe, possibly, she did penetration! It suddenly felt warmer in the library.

"So what's spelunking?" she asked, glancing at the book in my hand.

"It's exploring caves," I answered. And I blushed. Not a little pink blush, mind you, but a big, deep, purple blush.

She continued the conversation as though my face were a normal color. "Do you explore caves?" Smiling, she dragged the words out slightly.

"Well, I'd like to." My blush did not, would not, recede. My earlobes were throbbing.

"Caves have always fascinated me," she answered, again with the slightest drag on each word. She was flirting with me.

No, she was just chatting. Or was she? Her smile was lovely. Her eyes were dark and deep like a llama's.

The librarian said, "Next," and I paid my fine and left the library, too scared to look back for the woman in the fedora. But outside the library, I stopped. I didn't want to leave without talking to her some more. While I was frozen, deciding what to do, she came out.

Casually, as though we had known each other for years, she asked, "Want to get a cup of coffee?"

We settled into a booth in the back of a dingy coffee shop and quickly established that, yes, we were both lesbians, and, yes, we were flirting. Her name was Jesse. She was a poet.

After we had discussed Emily Dickinson and Adrienne Rich, she asked me if I had ever been in a relationship. I told her about Terry and our wonderful two weeks. I told her about my dates. Something in Jesse's face made me feel like I could tell her anything — or maybe I was just bursting to talk. But the next thing I knew, I was telling her about my desire to spelunk. She laughed. "What an utterly charming word," she said.

"You don't think it's male-identified?" I asked.

"Honey," she replied. "I don't give a shit what men do. I don't give a shit what anyone does. And I don't need a decoder ring and membership papers to be a lesbian. I do what I like."

She paused. "And I'm just crazy about spelunking."

I was ready to go home with her on the spot. Hell, I was ready to marry her. But she wanted to go slower.

"I'm an old-fashioned sort of gal," she explained. (Gal! Terry would have had a fit.) "How about we date a bit and see if we actually like each other?"

We dated. I learned that Jesse was not a separatist, not a butch, not a femme, not anything you could label. She was forty-five and had been a soldier, a nurse, and a sculptor. She wore fedoras because she liked them. She liked books, adventures, funny clothing, food. She liked almost everything, it seemed. Except rules.

We went to the movies. We held hands while Woody Allen and Diane Keaton battled a lobster, and Jesse drew little circles on my palms. I went home and masturbated. We went to a cheap bar, listened to jazz, drank beer, and sat shoulder to shoulder. I went home and masturbated. We took a long walk and made out in a quiet corner of the park. I went home and masturbated.

I had wild sex dreams. In one, I wore a miner's helmet, with the headlight pointed into Jesse's giant glistening cave. In my sleep, I started to fuck myself; half awake, I finished, with a roaring, echoing orgasm.

One night, we went dancing at our local lesbian bar. At first, I was embarrassed to be seen with Jesse. In a sea of work shirts and jeans, her red Robin Hood blouse, purple troubadour pants, and ever-present fedora looked clownish. But after one slow dance, lost in her body, I saw how beautiful she really was. When the music ended, she drawled, "So, does tonight seem like spelunking weather?"

"Oh, yes!" I squeaked.

We tore off our clothing as soon as we closed her front door. We stumbled around her living room, kissing and clinging. We dissolved down to the carpet, then touched and licked every inch of each other. Somehow, without discussing it, we agreed to leave our deepest parts for last.

Finally I could wait no more; my insides were crying, "Fuck me, please!" But I didn't know how to ask out loud. Luckily, my hips did. They rubbed up against Jesse's leg like they would swallow the whole limb. Jesse murmured, "You sweet wanting woman," and put her hand between my legs. My lips fell open under her touch. She played with my opening, putting just the tip of her finger inside me and moving it almost imperceptibly. I moaned, half in pleasure and half in frustration. Jesse teased, "One must be very careful when exploring new caves," and moved her finger inside just the slightest bit more. I couldn't take it. I thrust myself at her hand until her finger was all the way inside me, and I rocked against her. She added another finger, and another, and fucked me with long rhythmical strokes. I stopped rocking and just experienced her fucking me. With each stroke, I felt my insides grow larger and brighter. Jesse was bringing starshine to my lonely cave. Soon I was rocking again, meeting Jesse's hand with big, lovely slurps. Still fucking me, Jesse leaned down and licked my clit, her tongue matching the rhythms of her fingers. An orgasm tore through my body.

Jesse lay down next to me, her fingers still inside me. "Lovely woman, lovely woman," she murmured again and again, while post-come warmth pervaded my body. She nibbled my shoulder, and I kissed the top of her head. We breathed in and out together quietly.

After a while, when I had regained enough use of my body to start stroking Jesse's thighs, she said, "Have you ever considered simultaneous spelunking?"

I hadn't, but it seemed a wonderful idea. While Jesse stayed inside me, I stroked between her legs. I was tentative about going further, but Jesse used her free hand to guide me. Two of my fingers slipped into Jesse, and I gasped with wonder as they were swallowed in sweet, soft, slippery heat. Her cave walls were swollen and smooth and strong. I understood that caves were holy places.

I stayed in her. She stayed in me. We rocked together in a jumble of arms and legs. I had never dreamed anything could feel so spectacular. A roller coaster of feeling looped through the track made by our intertwined bodies.

I was spelunking at last.

About the contributors

❖❖❖❖

SDiane Bogus, a performance poet, publisher, and professor of composition and literature, is forty-five years old, an Aquarian, a Buddhist, and a bulldagger. She has written six books of poetry and prose, including the 1991 Lambda Award finalist *The Chant of the Women of Magdalena*. She is part-owner of Woman in the Moon Publications and teaches at De Anza College in Cupertino, California. Her business partner and life companion is T. Nelson Gilbert.

Wendy Caster's writing has appeared in *Lesbian Bedtime Stories 2*, *Cats (and their Dykes)*, and *Silver-Tongued Sapphistry*. Her opinion column, "Double Mischief," is nationally syndicated; in 1989, Wendy won the Lesbian and Gay Press Association Award for Editorial/Commentary. Her novel is crawling along. Wendy lives in San Diego with her flutist lover, Liz, and their three cats.

Alana Corsini is a Manhattan-based novelist, poet, and fund-raising consultant for cultural organizations who is working on a short-story collection initiated by the writing of her piece for this volume.

Diane Ferry is a writer of short fiction and prose poetry, and is currently working on a M.F.A. in creative writing at Brooklyn College and living in Brooklyn, New York.

Lynne Yamaguchi Fletcher is a Japanese-American poet and a resurrected celebrant of the body.

Jane Futcher has written or edited several books, including the young-adult novels *Crush* (Alyson, 1981) and *Promise Not to Tell* (1991), and *Building Bridges: Exploring the Needs of the Lesbian and Gay Community* (1990). Besides working as a masseuse, a free-lance editor and writer, and an anti-homophobia consultant, she also teaches creative writing at World College West in Petaluma, California, and is editor and co-publisher of *The Slant,* Marin County's first lesbian/gay newspaper.

Catherine Houser lives on a small island off the southern coast of Massachusetts, where she is working on a novel.

Willyce Kim is the author of two works of fiction, *Dancer Dawkins and the California Kid* and *Dead Heat* (both from Alyson). She has also written three books of poetry — *Curtains of Light, Eating Artichokes,* and *Under the Rolling Sky* — and has just completed a poetry manuscript called *Declarations* and her third novel, *Gabriella.*

Michele LaMarca has been writing short stories, poetry, and plays since the age of seven. "Window-Shopping" is her first published work. She lives in New Jersey.

Dorothy Love lives and writes in Los Angeles, California.

Molly Martin is an electrician who has worked and fantasized in many attics and crawl spaces. An activist and founder of Tradeswomen, Inc., a grass-roots organization of blue-collar women, she is a past editor of *Tradeswomen* magazine and edited the anthology *Hard-Hatted Women: Stories of Struggle and Success in the Trades* (Seal Press, 1988). She is currently working on a book about gay siblings.

Pam McArthur is settled in Framingham, Massachusetts, with her life-partner, their soon-to-be-born child, and two cats. The primary passions in her life are women, horses, writing, and penguins. In her spare time, she works with Davenport Arabians — the most wonderful horses this side of Charlie, she says. Originally a poet, she has recently become an enthusiastic writer of fiction, as well, and has stories forthcoming in *Common Lives/Lesbian Lives* and *Cachet*.

Lesléa Newman is the author of eleven books, the newest being *Gloria Goes to Gay Pride* and *Belinda's Bouquet* (children's books; Alyson, 1991) and *Sweet Dark Places* (poetry; HerBooks, 1991). Her new novel, *In Every Laugh a Tear,* will be published by New Victoria Publishers in the fall of 1992, and she has just completed a book of short stories entitled *Every Woman's Dream*.

Donna Nowak is a free-lance writer who resides in New Jersey and frequents her former residence in Greenwich Village. Her work has appeared in a variety of entertainment, literary, and progressive magazines and newspapers. Currently she is at work on her first novel. In addition to writing fiction and nonfiction, she draws cartoons and takes extensive dance lessons. New Orleans is one of her favorite cities.

Patricia Roth Schwartz lives with her partner on Weeping Willow Farm in central New York, where they are starting an herb business. She is the author of *The Names of the Moons of Mars* (New Victoria), a Lambda Award–winning book of short stories. Her volume of humor, *She Who Laughs Lasts,* will be out in the spring of 1992, and her novel *The River Is Wide, The River Is Deep* is in progress.

Rita Speicher was founder of the Women's Writers' Center, Inc., and Freehand, Inc., arts centers for women. Currently, she is general manager of the Desert Palms Inn, a gay resort in Palm Springs, California. "Long Distance" is a selection from her novel *Healing Arts After Hours*.

Other books of interest from
ALYSON PUBLICATIONS

❏ **AFTERGLOW,** edited by Karen Barber.
Filled with the excitement of new love and the remembrances of past ones, *Afterglow* offers well-crafted, imaginative, sexy stories of lesbian desire.

❏ **CHOICES,** by Nancy Toder.
Choices charts the paths of two young women as they travel through their college years as roommates and into adulthood, making the often difficult choices all lesbians will understand. "Nancy Toder's first novel really is a classic lesbian love story. The outstanding thing about *Choices* is that it is a good story." —*Off Our Backs*

❏ **A FEMINIST TAROT,** by Sally Gearhart and Susan Rennie.
"Reading the tarot can be a way of understanding the conscious and unconscious reality surrounding a particular question or circumstance. In *A Feminist Tarot* you'll learn how the traditional tarot can be a women's tarot...a tool for self-analysis. *A Feminist Tarot* gives us entry to knowledge of ourselves that we must never lose." —*The Lesbian News*

❏ **THE FEMME MYSTIQUE,** edited by Lesléa Newman.
"Images of so-called 'lipstick lesbians' have become the darlings of the popular media of late. *The Femme Mystique* brings together a broad range of work in which 'real' lesbians who self-identify as femmes speak for themselves about what it means to be femme today." —*Women's Monthly*

❏ **HEATWAVE: WOMEN IN LOVE AND LUST,** edited by Lucy Jane Bledsoe.
Where can a woman go when she needs a good hot...read? Crawl between the covers of *Heatwave,* a collection of original short stories about women in search of that elusive thing called love.

❏ **THE LESBIAN SEX BOOK,** by Wendy Caster.
Informative, entertaining, and attractively illustrated, this handbook is the lesbian sex guide for the '90s. Dealing with lesbian sex practices in a practical, nonjudgmental way, this guide is perfect for the newly out and the eternally curious.

❏ **THE PERSISTENT DESIRE,** edited by Joan Nestle.
A generation ago butch-femme identities were taken for granted in the lesbian community. Today, women who think of themselves as butch or femme often face prejudice from both the lesbian community and the straight world. Here, for the first time, dozens of femme and butch lesbians tell their stories of love, survival, and triumph.